The Man from Snowy River

The Man from Snowy River

Elyne Mitchell

*All characters in this book are
entirely fictitious, and no reference
is intended to any living person.*

Unit 4, Eden Park, 31 Waterloo Road,
North Ryde, NSW, Australia 2113, and
16 Golden Square, London W1R 4BN,
United Kingdom

This book is copyright.
Apart from any fair dealing for the
purposes of private study, research,
criticism or review, as permitted
under the Copyright Act, no part may
be reproduced by any process without
written permission. Inquiries should
be addressed to the publishers.

First published in Australia
by Angus & Robertson Publishers in 1982
Reprinted 1982 (twice)
This Eden paperback edition 1988

Copyright © Angus & Robertson Publishers and Snowy
River Production & Distribution Pty Ltd 1982

ISBN 0 207 15871 1

Printed in Australia by The Book Printer

Contents

Chapter One
BLACK BRUMBY STALLION
1

Chapter Two
TWO GRAVES AND AN EMPTY HUT
11

Chapter Three
"HE WAS WORTH A THOUSAND POUND"
23

Chapter Four
THE GIRL, THE LARRIKIN AND THE TOM FOOL KNOT
35

Chapter Five
"I HAVE NO BROTHER"
47

Chapter Six
SHARED SECRET
55

Chapter Seven
THE STALLION AND THE COLT
69

Chapter Eight
"AS DECEITFUL AS YOUR MOTHER"
83

Chapter Nine
ON THE CLIFF IN THE WIND AND THE SNOW
93

Chapter Ten
AN ENCHANTED SNOW GUM GROVE
105

Chapter Eleven
"I HARDLY RECOGNISED YOU WITHOUT YOUR GUN"
119

Chapter Twelve
"AND HAD JOINED THE WILD BUSH HORSES"
133

Chapter Thirteen
"CLANCY RODE TO WHEEL THEM"
145

Chapter Fourteen
"THE MAN FROM SNOWY RIVER"
155

Chapter One

Black Brumby Stallion

The cold autumn wind blew over the mountain peaks. It touched the hides of the wild horses, lifted the jet black and silver manes that shone in the sunset light. The sound of the wind in the granite tors, high above them, filled the mob with urgent disquiet.

The great black stallion tossed his head, gathered his herd, and set off at a wild gallop along the snowgrass ridge. The wind played with the horses, blowing the fluffy seeds of summer's golden billy buttons among their pounding legs, swaying the last remaining creamy candles of the candle-heath in the sphagnum bogs, so that the herd leapt and shied. Tails flew, hooves pounded on the snowgrass, and, with the thud and thunder of their galloping, excitement grew in the mob—passing like wildfire from stallion to mares, from the mares to the foals, to the fillies, to the young colts.

Whither away? Only the oldest of the mares had ever been on this side of the range before, but that black stallion knew his way. Something had drawn him, called him, till he crossed the mountains again.

Down the horses thundered into the dwarf snow gums. But while they were still high in the world, amongst the air and the wind, with the far-flung mountains all around them, the stallion stopped on a high knoll where the snow gums had long ago been killed by fire. The ancient limbs of the trees, once wind-twisted and pressed low to the ground, were now bleached to silver, and there the herd's leader stood, and there he reared, black above the silver lace of trunks and branches, and he threw a wild neigh ringing. He trumpeted out his great stallion call proclaiming the might he had to bestow—all that was his at birth, all that he had made his, in a lifetime in this high, wild land of snow, and frost, and the blizzard winds.

For that black stallion had seen many winters, galloped across much hard snow—sunk into soft snow, ploughing through it in all its sparkling depth. He had seen the brilliant days of many summers and the pouring rain and steel-hard frosts of many winters; he had seen lightning cleave the sky and set the forest ablaze. He had been shaken by thunder rolling round those granite rocks, and he had known wind that tore away heart and soul—or bore the seed of life. The howl of the dingo was part of his life, and the wild screaming of the black cockatoos. He knew the pigmy possums who travel the mountains on the tracks that the broad-tooth rats make through the alpine scrub. The sparrow hawk of summer had often hovered above him and his herd, and sometimes the black-shouldered kite. All this he held as memories within him . . . and he had known the love and care of human beings—and had chosen the wild.

Any mare that heard his neigh ring out from that high knoll would heed his call and follow him, through snow or flood; any young horse that heard that summons would sense all the excitement of the boundless forest and the high, bare ridges against the sky, and would be moved to join him.

While his herd stamped and snorted, still trembling with pleasure from the gallop, he led off, more slowly now, down between the great pillars of the mountain ash forest.

A dingo howled, somewhere down in a deep gully. The

forest of mountain ash was barely lit by the last of the sunset. One stretch of a little creek that ran at the foot of the woollybutts reflected the sky, so that the sunset colours lay, translucent, on the forest floor. The tops of the trees were briefly silhouetted against the light.

Again from the deep, deep gully came the haunting howl of the dingo, echoing round the timbered ridges—sad, eerie, part of a world into which man rarely strays. Darkness closed in slowly, till only the reflection of stars moved in the creek waters.

The dark bulk of a hut stood in a large, cleared flat. As darkness fell, its shape melted into the night, except for the chinks of light that showed through its slabs and gleamed in its small, square windows. That ancient howl of the dingo sounded again, throwing echoes from rock to rock, crying sorrow, loss, and longing. In the night, the sparks from the hut's chimney flew upwards.

Another sound passed through the bush, and the usual rustlings quietened. Even the dingo was silent. A giant flying phalanger, near the top of the smooth trunk of a ribbon gum, stopped climbing and sat listening to the sound. Animal, or bird, or even bunyip—it was impossible to imagine what made that weird noise. The sound came again, and it came from the hut. It began to turn into some sort of melody.

It stopped, and there were human voices. The flying phalanger continued up the tree, a wombat moved ponderously over the forest floor, then the dingo howl echoed again and again, and the sparks flew upwards above the stone chimney.

Inside the hut, a man's voice said:

"I don't think you'll make our fortune with that harmonium, Jim."

After a few more bars of the tune, Jim answered, laughing:

"It might chase off the dingoes." He stood up, a fair boy of about eighteen, and gently ran his work-scarred but sensitive hands over the veneer surface of the instrument.

He looked across at his father. The spare, strongly

built man was sitting at the end of the table, not far from the wide, open fire. Ledgers and notebooks lay open on the old table. Henry Craig was smiling, but he said:

"It's the debt collectors that I'd like to see kept off."

He put an old horseshoe, as a paper weight, on top of a bunch of accounts, and his hand smoothed the page of the ledger.

"Well, they won't come all the way up here," Jim said, frowning.

"No, but we won't get stores or boots next time we go to town."

A log rolled in the fire. Henry Craig spoke again:

"No matter which way I figure it, nought and nought still equals nought."

He smiled at Jim and walked to the rough stone fireplace, pushing the log further back with his boot, creating a burst of sparks as he stood there, leaning his elbow on the mantelshelf. A smoke-stained old oilcloth with a scalloped edge covered the rough-hewn shelf.

"Why don't we get Bess in foal, and pick up some more brood mares, Dad?" Jim suggested. "Why not go in for horses, more? This country breeds good horses."

Henry moved his arm slightly; the fire glow emphasised his cheekbones and forehead and the shadows deepened the graven lines there. Then he took an old tea cannister from the shelf, flipped up its lid, stepped across the slab floor, and emptied it on to the table by the ledger. A single note fluttered out and a few pennies rattled on the wooden surface. Jim watched silently, his hand still caressing the polished casing of the harmonium.

"That's why not—nothing to buy mares with," Henry said, and moved to the stove to start ladling out stew. "If we want to keep this place, we'll have to go down out of the mountains for a bit, and take a job—mustering, or horse breaking, to earn something more than we can make off this land at present."

The silence was broken by the long drawn-out "qua-a-ark" of a possum. Up till then he had not even considered that they might have to leave the mountain and take work in the lower country. Most deeply, he did not wish to go.

Jim could feel the touch of a wind that was gently moving the streamers of bark on the tall mountain ash, fanning the leaves of the snow gums up above; as it entered the hut, it moved some of the papers stuck on the walls. For a second that faint drift of air brought the eucalypt scent of the ash leaves in through the chinks of the hut. He knew that only very rarely would a wind at evening carry that marvellous mountain scent down on to the plains that lay below them. But if they had to go down there . . . He took a deep breath.

Henry put two plates of stew down on the table, got knives and forks from a drawer. The fire seemed to go quiet, and the whisper of the wind ceased. He knew quite well that his wife's illness had cost a lot of money; that, and poor prices for cattle since, had left him badly in debt. He and Jim would simply have to earn more. It wouldn't be the first time that men had worked for wages to make it possible to hold the land they owned.

"If we hired out as a team, I reckon we'd do quite well," he said.

"Not as cooks." Jim looked at the stew with twinkling eyes, but his smile deepened. Yes, they could work as a team.

The chill of the night and the silence seemed to lessen. There was warmth in knowing that his father valued his ability to break in a horse, to cut out a beast on a cattle camp, and to find his way when riding unknown country. He gave a little sigh, like the wind stirring those long leaves on the trees around their mountain clearing, and then tried to look confidently at his father.

"We'd do best breaking in horses," he said, finishing his stew. He poured hot water from a billy into a tin bowl, and rinsed his plate, then sat down at the harmonium and tried to play again. The wheezing and discordance was even worse. At last he gave up, and sat staring into the gloom of the hut.

"Mum really could play this," he said, and his voice

betrayed an aching regret.

Henry moved restlessly. Three years sometimes seemed such a long time, and yet he still rode home to the hut expecting to find her, or turned to speak to her as if she were still at his side. Things had not gone very well since.

"Yes," he said. "She played beautifully."

Once again the silence outside was broken by the faint sound of the wind. This time it was in the higher peaks, just the trees murmuring.

A disturbed whinny came from the shed outside.

"Bess can't have liked your music." Henry was trying to sound cheerful.

Jim got up.

"I'll go and see that she is all right," he said. The shed was quiet again but he took down a lantern, lit it, and walked out.

It was cold outside. Jim shivered and drew in a deep breath, trying to fill himself with the scent of the mountain bush, but even the scent seemed to have faded, as though the bush were withholding itself. The wind had dropped for the moment, and there was no murmur in the trees on the high ridges, no whisper of stirring bark streamers. Jim was used to that feeling in the bush, of silent, age-old waiting, but tonight it was profoundly noticeable.

He walked into the shed, but neither of the animals there greeted him, neither whickered an answer to his soft-spoken words:

"Hi there, Bess. Hi, Bob, old feller."

Then the dingo howled—quite close.

Jim hung up the lantern. The light gleamed on both pairs of eyes, the mare's and the gelding's; it made the harness, hanging on its rough wooden pegs, throw grotesque shadows. He noticed that his father had left his rifle in its saddle bucket below the harness. The dark shapes of the animals blended with the gloom of the shed.

The two horses seemed tense, on edge. He spoke to them gently:

"Whoa Bess, steady girl, steady."

The mare moved nervously. Something, too, upset the

old gelding. Jim felt his own skin creeping, but he did not know why. Bess snorted; Bob stamped his hooves. Jim stroked Bess's nose, patted her neck. In the half light he could see that her nostrils were flaring and her ears flickering back and forth, listening. Her eyes stared, the whites very noticeable in the lantern light.

"Steady, old girl," he murmured again.

But suddenly he was nearly knocked backwards as she flung up her head and whinnied. The sound filled the slab and bark shed, filled it with wild, throbbing excitement, and yet a touch of fear, too.

She reared and plunged, and reared again, only just missing Jim with her flailing hooves.

Henry Craig came racing across from the hut, and the mare quietened briefly.

Jim was breathless.

"I reckon the dingoes set her off," he said to his father.

Into the momentary quiet, there sounded the piercing call of a stallion.

"Not wild dogs—wild horses," Henry muttered.

Now the mare was out of control, and there was nothing they could do except try to soothe her and keep away from her thrashing hooves. The gelding, too, was banging and crashing around in his stall.

That stallion's call had come from somewhere very close. Henry looked out of the shed and was sure he saw brumbies racing through the trees not too far away.

Jim managed to tie a rope on either side of Bess's headstall and tether her securely. Then he joined his father outside the shed. Suddenly the brumbies broke out of the forest, further up the ridge, their shadows flickering in the faint glow of moonlight, and, as the moon rose, that great, black stallion reared in silhouette against it.

Henry's voice was almost a whisper:

"It's been years since he ran on this side of the mountains."

Then Henry went quickly back into the shed to get his rifle. When he returned, the stallion was still there, standing on a clear crest of the ridge against the moon. Henry began to load his rifle.

"You're not going to shoot him?" Jim gasped. "Please, Dad, no!"

Henry answered sharply:

"He's only going to cause us grief . . . take our horses . . . He's caused great sadness before."

Yet, even so, the father hesitated. For how could he shoot a horse he knew had once been made a scapegoat—had once been a symbol of love, and sorrow, and jealousy, even death?

Jim was horrified. His mind raced quickly.

"But Dad, there are some good horses there. They'd be worth a fair bit."

"Caught and broken, they might," he replied grimly, raising his rifle.

"No!" shouted Jim.

Startled by this loud cry, the stallion vanished and his herd melted into the bush as quickly as they had come. Slowly Henry Craig unloaded his rifle, and sighed—perhaps with relief.

The two of them stood watching and waiting to see if the brumbies would appear again. In that stallion, magnificent against the rising moon, the father had seen one thing, and his son had seen another.

Jim saw a grand animal, rearing, free and wild; and, though a shiver went down his spine and his skin suddenly seemed to rise in goose flesh, as if something like fear had momentarily swept through the bush, his thoughts turned to how they could catch those horses and break them in, and how, by using the mares for breeding, they might not have to leave their mountain home.

In the stallion Henry saw only a terrible reminder of the past; he recalled an earlier time in the lives of the mountain men, the memory of which should have been buried beneath the snow, but which still lived on, just as that stallion lived on.

"They'd have to be good animals, Dad," Jim said. "You reckon that old stallion's a thoroughbred; his mares must have got away from mountain stations, or from parties riding through, or be daughters of escaped mares—and no one in this area has ever had useless horses. They must be good."

"Yes, they'd be from good mares all right, and not only from mountain stations," Henry said, and his voice was sad. "The horses that get away and run wild, even on the plains, always make for the dense bush."

"We could catch them," Jim pleaded. He was trying to excite his father's interest and enthusiasm.

"Hold on, son," Henry smiled. "That horse has been running free since you were a small child . . . a magnificently cunning animal."

Jim forgot that little wind of fear blowing through the bush. Ideas and visions began to flow through his head. He had broken in quite a number of horses, and he imagined himself breaking in the brumbies from this thoroughbred stallion's mob.

"We could build a holding yard, up on the flat spur, and drive them in," he urged.

His father laughed. "You don't give up easily, son—I'll give you that." Nonetheless he was thinking, wondering if it were worth a try—even if only to please Jim. "No—I don't think so."

"But, Dad—"

"No," his father said firmly. "We'll yard them on Kelly's Saddle."

Jim gave a whoop of joy.

With the mare and gelding safely tethered, and quieter, now, the two walked back through the cold, moonlit night. The fire in the hut had died down to red coals and ash. Feeling tired, they did not even boil the billy for tea, but went straight to bed.

When the moon shadows had already crept round till they were pointing from north to south, Jim half woke. A vision of that stallion's head and its strong, noble body filled his waking dream; and in his ears his father's voice was saying: "He will only bring grief."

Something had disturbed his sleep and he was

shouting: "You're not going to shoot him?" Or was he shouting? For he had not woken his father.

He found himself whispering now: "That beautiful horse could not bring grief." And, in the dark of the night, enveloping him like a dream, came the thought that the black stallion symbolised in his magnificence night and day, life and death, grief and joy.

Then, suddenly fully alert, Jim knew that what had really woken him was a far-away chorus of neighs, and Bess answering it with longing.

He pulled his kangaroo skin rug right up over his chin, determined that Bess should not join the brumbies. But there again were the wild horses calling, calling through the night, and there was Bess's answer ringing out.

Chapter Two

Two Graves and an Empty Hut

A thin mist drifted over the mountain peaks, licked upwards hiding a rocky tor, moved through the snow gums, crept hither and thither down the corridors between the mountain ash. It wreathed about the rugged walls of a steep gorge, then rose, leaving the granite rocks, and flowed over Kelly's Saddle.

It was too thin a mist to deaden the sound of axes. The chopping rang out, sharp in the cold air. A pair of magpies carolled to the early morning.

Through the eddies of mist on the saddle could be seen rails already forming wings, and the start of a holding yard being constructed.

The chopping went on. Henry Craig and Jim were alternating, chop for chop, one on either side of a mountain ash that stood on the steep fall of the saddle. Bess was tethered not far away, her saddle on a log beside her; the gelding stood in logging harness, ready to drag logs into place.

Jim was exuberantly happy: his scheme to catch and yard the brumbies had been adopted. He and his father, working in unison, stopped and changed sides of the tree without either of them having to say a word to suggest they should change around.

Henry had an amused glint in his eyes. Jim was always a good worker, though at his best with horses, but he was so anxious to make these yards quickly that nothing would tire him. Henry enjoyed the rhythm of swinging an axe; he enjoyed the sound of it chopping into the wood, and the smell of the fresh-cut tree . . . It was really only because Jim, with his sensitivity to horses, made such a good job of breaking them in that Henry had agreed to the idea of catching the brumbies . . . He only wished he could rid himself of the faintly uncomfortable feeling that there had always been something unlucky about that thoroughbred stallion . . .

Henry had been born in the mountains, one of the earliest of the babies born to British settlers near the Snowy River. Though he had worked for a while on the Overflow, he had owned this piece of Snowy River country since well before Jim was born, and had done much felling of tall timber in the forests.

They stopped for a moment, before the final strokes that would fell the tree. Standing there, with the trees towering high above them, Jim laughed as he heard a lyrebird way down in the gorge below, mimicking the sound of their axes: "Chop, chop," it went, and then it whistled as a man would whistle his dog.

"Even a lyrebird is mocking us," Henry said. "It knows we do not need a sapling of this size to fence in a brumby."

"It was you who said that stallion would take some holding," Jim retorted with a grin, and looked approvingly at what they had already constructed—wings that would narrow down into a funnel and force a galloping mob of horses into the holding yard.

"Oh well," Henry said, "better to be certain. Perhaps the bird's only teasing us for trying to work so fast."

They went on chopping until the tree began to creak and groan, and then they stood clear for it to fall. With a great crack, a second of silence, and then that sudden rushing sound that falling timber makes through the air, the tree was down at last.

Jim began to hitch the gelding to the log. For once, he was too preoccupied to notice the warning that the bush birds and animals might have given him, and he did not heed Bess snorting and tossing her head. Henry, absorbed in his work as well, stood below the log. "Keep a strain on her, Jim," he called out.

Not far away, passing through a little clearing, the wild horses paced slowly, one after the other. They made barely any sound on the soft ground. Only the magpies saw the stallion's coat, all spangled with mist and shining in the early sun, as the currawongs gave voice to the excitement of seeing twenty horses or more.

"Up, up," Jim urged Bob, smacking the long reins down on the gelding's rump to encourage him. Only a small part of the boy's mind took in the excited singing of the currawongs. The gelding was leaning right into the traces, haunches straining as he pulled and pulled uphill. His muscles bulged under his sweating hide.

Suddenly there was a wild, high-pitched whinny from where Bess stood, and the air around them was filled with the sound of her hooves on stones, as she plunged and pulled back.

The gelding slackened his effort with surprise. Jim yelled at him, spanking the reins on his rump again, but Bob's hooves slipped, getting no purchase on the hillside. Jim slipped himself, but scrambled up to run to Bess who, tethered to a small tree by her bridle only, was pulling back, her hooves dug in, flinging her head from side to side to free herself.

"Quick, keep Bob at it. Hold the strain," Henry shouted, his voice full of urgency.

Jim rushed back to the gelding to urge him upwards. Horrified, he saw one link in Bob's drag chain opening and he started to shout a warning. Just then Bess's reins snapped. She fell as they gave, then the mare sprang up.

Henry glanced towards her for a fleeting second as she broke free, and then looked up the hill again towards the log. He stood transfixed. The chain had now parted, and the log was hurtling down the slope straight at him. With a big tree trunk lying behind him, he could not get out of its way.

Suddenly the whole bush was filled with a terrible sound as Henry's scream blended with the crashing of the log through the hop scrub. At this moment the herd of brumbies exploded from the bush with a thunder of hooves and wild neighing, and the black thoroughbred stallion gathered Bess into his mob and then at a fast gallop led the horses off.

Horror engulfed Jim—a nightmare of sight and sound—as he stood there transfixed, unable to move on that slippery slope. There was the weird, spinning picture of a breaking chain, of the log rolling straight on to his father, of horses galloping; there was the noise of a scream and the crash of timber, and then that ominous thunder of hooves . . . the stallion who would only bring grief . . . As Jim tried to run to his badly injured father, his feet kept slipping.

The log, having passed right over Henry Craig's body, was still rolling, crashing, bounding down the hill; finally, Jim knew by a tremendous splash that it had gone into the river below. It did not matter now, nothing like that mattered any more, and yet part of Jim's mind registered that the log would be carried down that stream and, unless it got snagged along the way, would ultimately join the Snowy River.

Even while half his mind took that in, the boy had reached his father's side. Henry was lying staring at the sky. Jim stopped still, almost in mid-stride. Till that moment he had not fully realised how badly his father was hurt. But now he saw the bloodied face and head, and heard the laboured breathing.

Jim bent over his father, horror, fear and desperate anguish all tearing at him. If only he hadn't almost demanded that they build the yards . . . if only he had not gone to Bess . . . if only he had seen that link parting earlier . . .

"I should have put a bullet into that stallion when I had the chance," Henry gasped out.

Jim was almost gabbling with fear:

"I'll . . . I'll get help . . . I'll get you down to Spur's place . . ."

If only Spur were here. Good old Spur—the luckless gold-miner—their nearest neighbour . . . Bess had been lent to them by Spur, and now Bess was gone.

Jim had to hold back a cry of anguish and fear as he saw a spasm of pain grip his father, saw the pain followed by a strange look of amazement.

"I won't be going anywhere, son," Henry whispered.

Jim shook his head desperately:

"I'll get you down," he vowed. But as he straightened up to go and get Bob, and saw the trampled ground again, the bent and broken scrub, he realised there was no horse standing nearby. Then he saw the gelding lying on his side, one leg obviously broken.

Jim turned back to his father.

"Bob's leg's broken," he said. "I'll have to shoot him."

Jim felt as if he were being forced on and on through this terrifying nightmare. If only he had not suggested that rather too large mountain ash . . . If only . . .

Henry's voice was steadily weakening.

"Do it now," he whispered, and then added: "Where's Bess?"

Jim, with his whole body shaking, wished that it were he who was going to die. His voice barely sounded:

"She's run off with the brumbies."

Henry closed his eyes.

"We've not one horse," and his whisper was like a sigh, for to be horseless in the high country was to be truly undone. "So, the brumby stallion has finally taken her away," he thought. "Old Spur won't take too kindly to that," he said more loudly, and then went on: "Ah, Spur and me—we had lots of dreams . . . and good times."

For Jim it was yet another terrible experience to have to shoot the old gelding. As he heard that fatal shot echo round the hills, he tried to stop his hands shaking, to still his fears and fight back an overwhelming feeling of remorse. He knew he should try to get his father into a more comfortable position, but Henry was in terrible pain.

As Jim covered his father with his jacket, the injured man at last spoke again:

"It's up to you, now, Jim."

His breathing seemed to be getting more and more laboured, so that Jim dared not leave him to go for help. That faint voice went on:

"This Snowy River country might not seem like much," and suddenly the old fire and vigour, the immense pride burnt in his father's face again, "but I wouldn't swap it for ten thousand acres down on the flats."

Jim looked away for a moment, at the tall trees and the tangle of snow gums a little higher up the spur; as he turned back, his father's head seemed to drop sideways, his hand lost its grip on Jim's and all of the man's tremendous effort to hold on faded. A currawong cried high in the sky and then that ancient silence filled the bush, until Jim's despairing cry rang out.

Blizzards and beating rain, frost and snow, burning sunshine and, so often, the wild winds—all this had been Jim's for all the eighteen years of his life. In the sudden blizzard of life that had now engulfed him, he was alone.

A flock of silver-eyes flew over and he heard their high whistling as they migrated north for the winter. Later in the day he saw four ducks winging high above, their necks outstretched.

Jim stayed a long time beside the body of his father before stumbling off through the bush to find Spur.

A few days later Jim stood alone beside two graves: his father's, freshly dug, with the rough-hewn, wooden cross which he had placed over it, to mark it until he had the money to buy a headstone; and his mother's. He and his father between them had kept her grave free of weeds, and planted it with sarsaparilla, with golden and white everlastings and some mauve eye-brights. "Ellen Mary Craig" was on the ornate headstone. "Departed this life May 1885. Gone with God." On the makeshift wooden cross Jim had painted: "Henry Craig. Died of Accident 1888."

The minister had come and gone; he had read the Service for the Burial of the Dead and ridden away again. The few mountain men who lived close enough, and who had known Henry Craig as a boy or man were leaving. For Jim there had been the quite unbelievable finality of the coffin lowered into the grave, and of the earth covering it. Now he stood there deep in thought.

Six of the mountain men who had not yet left were talking, almost arguing together, on their horses by the hut. Spur, in his spring cart, drove up beside Jim.

"What a tragedy," the old man said, looking down at the graves.

Jim, trying to hold himself together, answered very quietly:

"United in death, the minister said."

"Superstition!" Spur growled.

"It's a nice thought, all the same."

"A great comfort for widows and fools. There's more to life than death, boy."

Jim had often wondered what experience in life had made Spur rather "agin everything", but just then he saw the six mountain men turning towards him on their horses. They rode up in a grim silence broken only by the gang-gangs raucously grumbling in the trees nearby and throwing down cracked and broken gum-nuts. Jim knew these men—particularly Jake, their leader—but not very well. He was totally unprepared when Jake said:

"Well, that's it, lad. You can't stay here."

Jim had been planning to go down to stay with Spur, at least for a while, but this statement seemed unbelievable.

"But it's my place, now," he said, and when Spur said no word in support, he almost shouted:

"I own it."

"Owning's got nothing to do with it. It's who can make a go of it, up here." Jake spoke harshly.

"I can look after myself," Jim said, but his confidence was not very great, and the six, rock-hard faces of the old mountain men made him feel uncertain.

"Maybe . . . one day," Jake said, looking down at the crude wooden cross.

Jim was hurt and angry.

"What gives you the right . . ."

"Look here!" Jake's voice was harsher than the gang-gangs as he raised a hand in fierce command. "You go down to the low country and earn the right to live up here, just like your father did."

The six horsemen, clad in their oilskins, did not even give Jim a chance to answer. Looking like prophets from the Old Testament, they turned their weather-carved faces away from him and rode off.

Jim, with tears beginning to prick his eyes, tried to keep his lips steady. He looked back at his hut, empty and lifeless—with not even a horse tied up at the rail—and back again to the graves.

Knowing what must be done, he walked quickly over to the hut, stepped across its threshold and picked up his swag. He took one last look around—at his mother's pictures, her box of pressed wildflowers, her music, her drawings, the books from which she had given him his school work—and then he turned, walked out, and bolted the door. He put the swag into Spur's spring cart and went round to the harness shed for his saddle, his bridle and his whip. When he had put them in the cart too, he swung up beside the old man.

"Let's get going, Spur," he said, trying to conquer his mounting misery and to keep his voice steady.

Spur looked more like a scarecrow than a mourner returning from his best friend's funeral, with his clothes hanging off him and his ancient hat pulled down over his rather crazy eyes, but he flicked the reins furiously, and they rolled away, gathering speed, soon going at his accustomed dangerous pace.

The track was rough and sometimes barely visible. They rocked their way along it, over stones, over branches that had fallen, over mounds and into hollows, their heads and shoulders brushed occasionally by gum leaves or the fronds of wattle. They swept round a bend, narrowly missing the trunk of a ribbon gum, and there, ahead, before the trees blocked the view again, was the southern wall of the Snowy Mountains—great, piled-up rock peaks, sharp rock ridges, clefts carved out by roaring streams, huge snowgrass basins, and steep rock bluffs above drops of thousands of feet—the Ramshead Range.

Jim stared at the mountains.

"They blame me for Dad's death, Spur," he said and, though *he* also blamed himself, he really could not see how those men could. A link of the chain had parted, causing the log to roll. "I reckon I've got a lot to live down."

"A hard country makes for hard men," was Spur's answer, but only he knew all the events that had led to this tragedy, events a long time ago, in which he himself had played a part. It was not only Henry's death that had been a disaster.

"You've got a damned sight more to live up to," Spur added as he yelled at his horse again: "Come on! Get up!" and they sped on through the bush, rocking from wheel to wheel.

They thundered through a creek, a bow wave in front of them and an enormous, spraying wake behind. Jim hung on, and checked that his saddle and swag were still aboard. It momentarily crossed his mind, as the cart bounded from bump to bump, flew across logs, and tilted one way and then the other, that they too might finish up more dead than alive.

At last Spur's hut was in sight. Jim knew it well, but, as they skidded round a big black sallee and Spur pulled the horse up on its haunches, so that they nearly shot out over the dashboard, he seemed to notice the topsy-turvy architecture even more than usual, perhaps because it was such a contrast to the hut which he had just locked and left.

His father's hut had only been added to twice: once when Ellen Mary had come to live in it, and once when Jim himself was born. Spur's hut had rooms added on everywhere, and verandahs tacked around, with no planning visible. Equipment for mining, for fencing, for fishing all hung around its slab walls; harness and whips, branding irons for cattle, great-jawed dingo traps—endless bits and pieces everywhere. And there was the usual shelf carrying a tin basin for washing with rough buckets stacked underneath.

Jim swung out of the cart. As Spur leapt out too, springing up on to the porch and kicking the door open with his wooden leg, Jim smiled wryly—even a wooden leg couldn't restrain Spur's bounce. Jim rarely noticed this handicap of Spur's because he always seemed to turn it to advantage.

Jim led the horse round to the back of the main hut, where there was a bark lean-to for the spring cart. He unharnessed the horse, brushed the sweat out of his coat and put some chaff and bran in an old trough for him. Then, rather dragging his feet, Jim went back towards the hut.

Ever since he had been a very small boy, Jim had been fascinated by the intricacies of Spur's hut, with all its wire and string devices, and by Spur's own jack-in-a-box activities. But just now he felt he could do without the weird mechanics and the leaping around, even though Spur had always been his own good friend and his father's mate.

Jim went in through the door and stood awkwardly, waiting to be given a job to do. Spur simply looked at him without expression, and went on stirring a very large stew pot. At last he spoke:

"Spur's famous wallaby stew, spoken of in hushed and reverent tones over the length of the Great Dividing Range," he said, ladling it into two bowls and setting them down on the rough table. "Do you feel up to sharing some with me?"

Jim shook his head, indicating his lack of hunger.

"Oh well, famous indeed!" Spur grinned. "Word must have got around—even my dogs are wary of it." He began to make tea in a billy.

Jim, with his untouched bowl on the table in front of him, suddenly spoke in a low voice, as though they had just been talking about Henry:

"He used to talk of you taking the harmonium up the mountain."

Spur laughed.

"Your mother's music box. Your father and me got it up there without a scratch. By the way, how's that mare, Bess?"

Jim looked hard at the bowl in front of him:

"She went off with the brumbies, Spur." As the old man looked at him in utter surprise, he added:

"The old thoroughbred's mob, the big black."

Spur stared unseeingly at the hessian walls, and at the newspaper pasted on to the hessian to keep the draughts out. At last he said:

"I remember that animal."

Jim was too taken up with his own unhappiness and sense of failure to see the sadness in Spur's face.

"I'll get her back," he said, "I'll get her back somehow."

At this Spur laughed cynically:

"Sure you will. You'll just walk in and pluck her out of a thousand square miles of wilderness."

"I will," Jim said. "I will somehow. I'll run down that mob one day and get her back."

Spur gave the boy a mocking look:

"Sure!" he said. "And all on foot too!"

Jim looked across at Spur, his expression woebegone. The realisation that he was now a horseman without a horse struck him like a hammer blow.

Spur sat drinking his tea for a few minutes, watching

Jim trying to swallow his but almost choking. When their pannikins were empty, the old man spoke gently:

"Come on. I've something to show you."

At an astonishing speed, he led the way out of the hut and through a stand of candlebarks to his yards. It was sunset; the oblique light picked out the red in the candlebarks and shone on the bleached rails—throwing a glow over the hide of a small, wiry, dun-coloured horse that stood in the yard. It had its head up and its ears pricked.

Spur walked to the rails.

"I've no notion of his breeding. But he is a mountain horse, a good one. He's called Andy and he's yours."

Jim frowned:

"But Spur, I can't pay you for him."

"He's not for sale," the old man replied firmly.

Jim was embarrassed:

"Now, hold on, Spur," he muttered.

"Don't argue." Spur looked fierce. "A man without a horse is like a man without legs."

Jim slipped through the rails, looked appraisingly at the horse, and put his hand out, murmuring quietly. Andy extended his nose, sniffed the hand, and came a little closer. Jim found himself looking at a proud animal who looked straight back at him. Then Andy moved forward, with complete trust, and rubbed his head against Jim's chest.

"Ah," said Spur. "See, he's claimed you."

"Thank you very much, Spur." Jim found his voice unsteady again. "I could get your Bess back again, now."

"Forget Bess," Spur said quite fiercely. "Forget that brumby mob. Don't throw effort after foolishness, and perhaps ruin a good horse doing it. That stallion brings only sorrow."

Jim moved closer to the small horse and rubbed his face on its neck. It was strange . . . Spur had used almost the same words as his father.

Andy nuzzled his head.

Chapter Three

"He Was Worth a Thousand Pound"

Jim had never seen the town so full of people before. There were men and women on horseback, in spring carts, in jinkers, in buggies and buckboards, even whole families in wagons. Admittedly, he and his parents had not gone to town often, for it was quite a long way from their mountain holding, but he knew that a crowd like this was an unusual sight.

Along with the people from the bush, the townsfolk were hurrying down the main street. Most of the shops seemed to be closed. It had just stopped raining and all the horses and vehicles and people on foot were trying to avoid the puddles.

Jim rode Andy down the street, splashing in the potholes and wondering what was causing all the excitement.

Four men hurried along on foot in front of him; they were trying to keep up with a tall, lean, elderly man who was walking too fast for them. One of the four, a flash-looking fellow, was talking hard to the tall man, but he seemed to take no notice.

As Jim drew level with them, he heard the flash-looking man say:

"Mr Harrison, for you I'd come down to two guineas a head." Then, seeing that made no impression, he added: "Well, pounds then."

The striding man, addressed as Harrison, answered at last:

"Listen, I've got other things on my mind today."

Jim heard one of the four growl: "Damned Yankee," and he saw Harrison's lean, arrogant face under some thick, white hair and a wide-brimmed hat.

Other people were calling out greetings and good wishes to Harrison. To them he responded courteously, if absentmindedly.

Jim looked down at the man who had been trying to make a deal.

"Who is that?" he asked.

The flash man answered:

"Are you from the back blocks or somethin'? Don't you know Harrison? Don't you know that he's pickin' up his colt today? They say it's worth a thousand pounds."

Jim gasped.

"A colt? . . . A colt worth a thousand pounds?"

"Yeah." The flash man was glad to have made an impression on someone. "That's why the bloody town's so full. Everyone rushin' to the railway yards. The train'll be in any minute."

Even as he spoke, the sound of a train's whistle came from quite close and the movement of vehicles, horses and people in the street became even more frenzied. Women, with long skirts trailing in the mud, were pulling along little girls in frocks that reached to their black-buttoned boots, and small boys in sailor suits or knickerbockers. Even dogs were hurrying to the scene.

Jim was not going to miss seeing a colt that was reputed to be worth a thousand pounds, so he found an unoccupied hitching post, tethered his horse securely to it, and joined in.

The rain started again, just as the train, billowing steam, pulled up at the station. A man in a bowler hat, dressed as though for the city, was standing in the open doorway of one compartment as the train squeaked and blew to a halt.

The crowd, with umbrellas held high and oilskin coats dripping, parted to let the commanding figure of Harrison get through. The city man sprang down from the iron step of the train compartment and took Harrison's outstretched hand.

"Glad to see you, Paterson," Harrison said. "I'm sorry about this blasted circus." He waved his hand at the crowd.

"Well, no wonder really. The colt is already famous and he's a fine animal," Paterson answered.

"So he should be, for the price! As old Regret's last foal, he's irreplaceable. I'm most grateful to you for bringing him."

Paterson laughed.

"Anything to get away from the city—especially when it's to bring you the finest colt in the colony."

Jim tried to force his way through the milling crowd and follow the two men as they walked up to the covered stock wagon. He had almost forgotten all his sorrows in his eagerness to see this famous colt. And somehow, somewhere, a long time ago, he had heard that name "Regret".

The crowd was beginning to get excited, and there was a continuous murmur of voices, of children crying, and dogs snapping and growling. Both Harrison and Paterson waved everyone back as a young stockman with a big hat and oilskin coat directed two men who were unfastening the latches on the wagon door.

The door came down with a thump, sending up a great splash of mud. Once down, it became a ramp on which the colt could be led out.

Jim could hear the colt stamping and plunging inside. He wriggled through the crowd, right up to the front, and saw the young stockman run up the ramp and disappear inside.

Harrison strode forward, calling into the wagon:

"Take your time, Jess." Then he turned to the crowd:

"Get the dogs out of the way, and the kids," he commanded, and both he and Paterson went to stand one on each side of the ramp. The stamping and plunging in the wagon ceased, and even the crying children and snarling dogs became hushed and expectant.

Then there came the sound of hooves clattering over the wagon floor. Jim knew that the great moment had arrived, but he was momentarily anxious that too many people, children and dogs were crowded around, and too tightly packed. After all, a thoroughbred colt was to be respected—and a colt could cause injury in such a confined space.

He saw the slight figure of the stockman backing out of the wagon door, obviously talking quietly to the colt which he was leading. Then at last the colt appeared, and stood for a moment as though exhibiting his own splendour. But Jim could tell that he was not showing off at all—he was simply a young horse feeling very nervous. As the stockman backed down the ramp, the colt followed, looking nervously at the crowd, the whites of its eyes showing.

Then it happened. A dog sprang up on the ramp and the colt jumped with fear. He knocked the young stockman over and began rearing and striking out with his hooves. Children were howling and screaming, the crowd pushing and shoving to get out of reach of the striking front hooves.

Two men rushed out of the crowd to try to catch the colt, but they only frightened him more. He reared high above them, thundering down with his front hooves, and swinging off to one side.

Harrison and Paterson both tried to grab the leading rein, and at the same time calm the crowd. Mud was flying and dogs were fighting among themselves, but the young stockman, still determinedly hanging on to the rein, was being dragged around in the mud.

Jim, having looked after horses all his life, automatically stepped forward. Pushing Paterson out of his way, he managed to catch the leading rein; then he started speaking quietly to this colt who was more beautiful than any horse he had ever seen or touched before.

"Whoa there, boy, easy now, take it easy," he murmured softly. Then, without turning, he spoke to the sprawled stockman:

"Let go, mate."

When the boy did not let go, thus making Jim's task more difficult, Jim became impatient and jerked the rein loose from his hand, saying:

"Let bloody go!"

Jim went on talking softly to the colt, stroking him with gentle hands, until he had him standing still, even if ready to jump at any moment. Once he had the horse quietened, he turned to tell the young stockman not to be such a fool—and his mouth gaped with disbelief. The "stockman" was a girl!

Even though her face was all muddied, and she dripped water from her tangled hair, he knew she was lovely. The words he was going to say had gone, leaving him speechless, his eyes wide open with surprise.

Harrison grabbed the leading rein out of Jim's hand, as if the boy did not exist, although in fact he had chosen not to intervene until Jim had completely quietened the colt.

"Are you all right, Jess?" Harrison asked anxiously.

The girl swept the mud off her oilskin and glared at Jim.

"If I'd needed your help, I'd have asked for it," she spat out, turning her back and walking away with Harrison and the colt.

It was Paterson who saved Jim from uncomfortable embarrassment.

"I think we are all indebted to young Mr . . ."

"Jim Craig," Jim answered and held out his hand, which Paterson immediately shook. But Harrison was already striding off with his thousand pound colt.

"Barty Paterson," the city man introduced himself, "and that was Mr Harrison, and," with a quizzical look towards Jessica's angry departing back, "that was his charming daughter, Jessica."

Jim stared after Harrison and his daughter as they walked away out of sight. Strange, he thought—old Harrison reminded him of someone . . .

"Mm . . ." he said, collecting himself. "Charming! . . . Are you a stock agent, Mr Paterson?"

Paterson laughed:

"No, as a matter of fact I'm a city lawyer. Though born and bred in the country, Jim. How about you?"

"I've just arrived in town."

Paterson turned to go:

"Well thanks again, Jim," he said. "If ever we can return the favour, let us know."

Jim realised that he must not let such an opportunity go.

"I'm looking for work, sir," he burst out, all in a rush.

Paterson looked thoughtful. "These are hard times, Jim," he said slowly.

"I know that." Jim spoke quickly and eagerly. "But I've got a place to keep up. I've lived on the land all my life, so I can turn my hand to almost anything. And, I've got a good stockhorse."

He stood there, in the muddy railway yard, young, anxious, but suddenly with the proud bearing of a mountain man.

"Have you, now?" Paterson chuckled. "Well, in that case, I suppose we'd better find you work . . . I'll give you a letter."

Jim was too grateful really to wonder about the odd, half-amused glint in Paterson's eye as the lawyer wrote a quick note, and handed it over. He was too confusedly grateful to take in immediately that the letter was addressed to Harrison.

Up in the mountains old Spur, stumping around on his peg-leg with his waistcoat flying and his ancient hat clamped down on his head, gave only an occasional thought to the lad gone to town to try and get a job so he could pay his debts and keep his mountain property. Spur's thoughts—or dreams—were mostly of his gold mine, and they had become weirder and wilder as the years went by, just as his appearance became more and more that of a "mad hatter".

On the day that old Regret's last colt arrived in town, Spur, utterly frustrated by his gold mine, was stumping back along it to the opening, with his lantern in hand, and was agilely negotiating all the puddles on the floor of the tunnel which had taken him twenty years to dig into the mountainside. As always, when on his own, he was talking to himself, or rather to the mine. The mine was female.

"I'll find it one day," he muttered. "I know it's hidden in your skirts somewhere, you damned trollop."

As if in reply, the old shoring creaked and groaned, causing a sprinkle of dust to shower down on to him. Cursing, Spur went on, making his way out through the mine's crazy leaning door, and then yelled back down the tunnel:

"You'll not trifle with me any more. I'll find it!" and he banged shut the door over which the name of the mine, Matilda, was painted.

As he started to padlock the bolt, Spur heard more earth falling inside and growled:

"You'd have the last word, wouldn't yer?"

Everything—the door, the shaft, the mullock heap, and a little shack that covered his explosives—was well camouflaged, hidden under wattle scrub or branches. The mine's whereabouts were a secret shared with no living soul, now that Henry Craig was gone.

Spur gave a nervous start: surely he had heard a horse snort? Alert, wild-eyed, he sprang off his one good leg towards his tethered horse and pulled an old pistol out of his saddle pouch. Then he crept towards the place from which that sound had come, his pistol cocked and on the ready.

A casual voice said:

"You going horse hunting, Spur?"

Spur wheeled furiously round towards the speaker. There, with a mocking grin on his face, and quietly filling his pipe, sat a man dressed neatly in stockman's moleskins and a brightly coloured shirt.

Spur's anger went off the boil.

"Damn you, Clancy. How'd you find this place?"

Clancy of the Overflow, stockman, horseman, first-class tracker, first-class drover, chuckled.

"I tracked you, you silly old galah. You leave a trail like a one-legged seed drill. Now, say you're glad to see me."

"Damn you, Clancy," Spur reiterated. "Always sneaking around, making no noise, surprising a fellow."

Clancy grinned as he started to light up his pipe.

"Could've sworn I heard voices up here."

Spur had recovered some of his jauntiness.

"Ha!" he jibed. "Sure sign of old age when you start hearin' things," and he went to check the padlock on the door, just once more.

"Are you and that partner of yours still looking for El Dorado?"

Spur kept fiddling with the padlock.

"Silent partner, now," he said. "Henry Craig's dead."

Clancy's face lost its mocking, teasing expression.

"Oh," he said quietly. "I'm sorry to hear that." Then he called his horse up out of the bush.

Spur loosed his own horse and leapt into the saddle in that swift and strange fashion of his while Clancy swung on to his flashy brown. A black packhorse followed the brown out of the trees so that a cavalcade of three went off through the trees towards Spur's house.

Spur was still thinking of Henry Craig.

"Dead," he said, "just when good colour was showin' up, too."

Clancy ducked his head under an overhanging wattle bough.

"You've been saying that for twenty years," he grinned.

Spur rolled his eyes:

"And I suppose you expect me to put food in your craw after enduring your jokes and insults?"

"Oh well," Clancy chuckled as he gazed through the tall, straight trunks to a distant crag. "You've promised me food for twenty years, too, and all I ever get is wallaby stew."

Outside Spur's incredibly crooked hut, Clancy sat himself on a log in the autumn sunshine amid the mountain trees, whose limbs and leaves mottled the tussocky snowgrass with their moving shadows. A mountain grasshopper, its wings a brittle, shining net of black and its back brilliantly banded with red and blue, caught his attention. At times like this he could appreciate the beauty of the mountains vividly enough to understand why a man like Spur could never bear to leave them.

Presently Spur himself came limping out of his hut, carrying two bowls of stew.

Clancy looked warily at the contents of his bowl.

"What is it?" he asked.

Spur did not have his mind on the question, but automatically answered:

"Wallaby stew. Tasty, eh?"

Clancy took a tentative half-mouthful.

"You ought to advertise it in *The Bulletin*," he said, putting his bowl down on the snowgrass by the log and accepting a pannikin of tea, "as a new, miraculous cure for appetite!"

"And to think," Spur rolled his eyes upwards, "that I was going to leave you a share of the mine . . ."

"Thanks very much," Clancy said courteously, "but I've my own rainbows to chase."

"Still in love with your sunlit plains," Spur chuckled, "your vision splendid . . ." The old man gazed out over the mountains. "Give me the wind soughing through the tall ash, or the snowflakes falling slowly past their trunks, separate flakes drifting down into a thick carpet of snow . . . and, o' course," he added quickly, "m' gold mine."

"Gold mine! At least I've got the sun and the stars

overhead. That's better than being in a dark tunnel, seeking something that isn't there."

Spur leapt up in one of his easily provoked passions and rushed back into the hut.

"Not there!" he cried, producing a jar and spilling its contents on to a bench top. "Take a look at this!" The crushed quartz showed glittering grains of gold, particles of gold reflecting the sunlight that streamed through the dry autumn air.

Clancy raised one eyebrow and smoothed his fingers over his well-kept moustache.

"Not much to show for twenty years, old timer. You must've dug a trench to California in that time."

Spur was prancing around on his wooden leg.

"This is much better than anything I ever saw there in '49. I've put a drive straight in for thirty chains. Now I go down, sink a shaft, and we'll be smack on top of the richest vein."

"Who's *we*, Spur?"

"Young Jim Craig. Henry grub-staked me for fifteen years, so the lad inherits his share. I'm not telling him yet, though. Better he makes his own way for a while."

"That," said Clancy, "is what I'd call a deep secret." He had a wicked gleam in his eye: "I thought you might have given it to your brother."

Spur's mood suddenly changed—becoming almost sour, almost angry:

"The only thing I'd give that lump of flint is a stick of dynamite with a short fuse."

While the old miner and the legendary stockman sat discussing the "deep secret", young Jim, with his letter from Paterson in his pocket, was riding towards Harrison's property.

The homestead was still in the distance, but the well-fenced paddocks, and the fat Herefords grazing peacefully there, had already made Jim a little uneasy. Sweet mountain pasture he knew and loved; this ordered plenty was something else entirely. He could tell it was good, well-managed, cared for, but somehow he just felt uneasy.

Then, when the homestead came clearly into view, he really began to wonder if this was the right place for Jim Craig from the Snowy Mountains. Automatically he slipped his hand into his pocket and drew out Paterson's letter. Yes, there it was, clearly addressed to Harrison. Then he recalled that his father never ran away from anything. Jim, too, had been reared never to run away.

He rode slowly through the cattle. That was another thing he had been taught—never to ride fast through fattening cattle, never to disturb them.

Gradually he came closer to the homestead. The main building seemed to be in several sections—perhaps even a man as well off as Harrison was not all that rich to start with, and added to his house as the mountain people did, Jim reflected.

He judged the house as very well built. It was of smoothly adzed slabs with rather high-pitched shingled roofs. There were verandahs with creepers climbing up the posts, a neat garden and lawn, and a large, gaunt eucalypt. Then Jim took in the yards and big stables close by, and a slab building that could be the station hands' barracks.

It looked like a place where a lot of work was always being done. Everything was incredibly neat, so the work was obviously done well. Presumably Harrison ruled everything and everyone here in the same way as he had at the railway yard—like a king.

When Jim got even closer, he saw there were cattle in some of the yards, and the beautiful colt from old Regret was in a yard on its own. Then he saw Mr Harrison leaning on a railing.

He rode right up, dismounted, and presented Harrison with the letter which Paterson had given him. Harrison's disdainful gaze—taking in not only him but his mountain horse too—was anything but encouraging.

"Are you from the high country?" Harrison asked, and when Jim said yes, Harrison, appearing to be even less impressed, looked at the letter from Paterson again. Paterson had recommended Jim; he owed Paterson something for escorting the colt.

"I'll give you a try," he said. "Usual wages and keep. Make yourself known to the foreman."

Jim nodded. But again the same nagging thought that had puzzled him in the railway yard came to him now. As Harrison walked away, he felt sure he had seen this man somewhere before.

"Thanks a lot, sir," Jim called out and moved off quickly enough not to hear Harrison mutter:

"Charity cases! Damn your eyes Paterson!"

But then the station owner turned and watched the colt:

"Ah, but you're a grand judge of horse flesh!"

Chapter Four

The Girl, the Larrikin and the Tom Fool Knot

Filling the kitchen woodbox was an easy task for Jim. Chopping snow gum and black sallee logs for the hut fire had been his job since he was big enough to handle an axe. But just now he had to work hard to push away the memories that sound—chop, chop, chop—brought flooding back: the chop, chop, chop that had echoed around in the mountain ash forest, the mocking mimicry of the lyrebird, the vision of his father's smiling face on the other side of the trunk as they worked as a team. He had to ward off the surging memory of his father's scream, the picture of the sliding, striking log . . . He had to work.

Jim filled the woodbox so quickly that Kane, the foreman, could hardly conceal his surprise as he hastily sent him to muck out the stables.

As he followed the boy out, Kane stopped at the back door to talk to Mrs Bailey, the cook.

"Hard worker," she said, nodding her head at Jim's back as he walked to the stables, "but I can't understand why the boss took him on. He comes from the mountains, you know."

"Oh well," Kane said, looking uneasy, "maybe that's

all too far in the past for the boss to worry about now."
His tone prohibited any more comment as he moved off.

Mrs Bailey remained standing there, gazing out at the blue, far distant mountains, remembering. What was done, was done, of course, but past events could never be just wiped off the slate, as it were, because she knew they caused events to happen even now and created certain attitudes of mind that made people the way they were.

Mrs Bailey had lived on this station homestead a great deal of her life, somehow close to the land and the basic elements of life even though she spent most days in the kitchen, and she knew that the passage of events, started so many years ago, was still relentlessly unfolding.

Jim found a shovel just inside the stable door, and looked around. The stables were solidly built of adzed slabs, like the homestead, but the effect was rougher. They were roomy, well-planned, easy to work. He started mucking out a stall next to one in which a nervous grey gelding was moving from one foot to the other. He took time off to stroke the gelding's nose and make friends with it, and then got on with the job.

He soon became aware of two young men approaching. Out of the corner of his eye, he could see that they were only a few years older than himself. He saw flashy waistcoats, polished boots, the jaunty angle of their hats, and a thought went through his head—they were not the type he would have expected a hard man, like Harrison, to employ.

The two stood and watched him work. Jim, feeling embarrassed, nodded and said:

"G'day. I'm Jim Craig."

The leader of the gang of two was rolling a cigarette:

"He's pretty good at shovelling that stuff, eh Moss?"

His big, gorilla-like follower, Moss, gave a silly giggle:

"Sure is, Curly."

Jim made sure he did not let his rising anger show.

"Pretty smart for a mountain fellow: he's learnt to use the flat end," Curly went on, and Moss laughed raucously.

Jim, flustered, drove the shovel hard into the earthen floor.

"See!" Curly grinned at Moss. "They live like bandicoots up there, in the mountains. I think he's digging for grubs. That right, Bandicoot?"

Doggedly, Jim worked on. The silence lengthened.

"Have they given you the day off?" asked Jim finally.

Curly flicked at an invisible thread on his coat as he put the cigarette to his lips.

"I'm studying to be a supervisor," he offered. "Isn't that right, Moss?" Lighting the cigarette, he dropped the match in some dry straw.

"Studying to be stupid," Jim said, and he carefully emptied a shovelful of fresh manure on to the burning straw and over Curly's polished boots. He had met, and dealt with, Curly's type before.

As they glared at each other, the sound of light footsteps approached. Jessica Harrison, dressed for riding, walked briskly into the stables.

Curly's manner changed completely.

"Good morning, Miss Jessica," he said in an ingratiating tone. "Would you like me to saddle up Kip for you?"

"No thank you," she answered rather shortly.

Curly motioned to Moss for them to go.

"Well, I'll be getting about my duties," he said and, turning to Jim, patted him on the shoulder. "You're getting the hang of it, son. Keep it up. I'll be back later to check on your work."

Jim had felt sufficiently shy at Jessica's arrival without the added embarrassment of seeing her amusement at Curly making a fool of him. He busied himself at his raking, to hide his anger and hurt, and did not realise that Curly was still hanging around, watching through a window, or that Jessica's gelding, Kip, was more restless than usual.

Jessica found that the headstall on Kip was broken, and Kip would not even hold his head still for her to take it off. Jim heard her admonishing Kip, saw the broken headstall, and saw her take a coil of rope from a peg. Rather on the defensive—not having forgotten her highhanded treatment of him in the railway yard—he offered to help.

"No, I'll manage," she replied curtly.

He kept on raking, but saw her attempt to make a halter out of the rope fall apart and the gelding start to rear. Quickly Jim took the rope from her hands and made a double loop; letting the loops drop, he pulled his hand through and had a halter on the gelding's head in an instant.

Jessica was staring at him, barely believing what she had seen.

"Show me how you did that," she demanded, but her voice was friendly.

"Easy." Jim had forgotten his embarrassment. He took another coil of rope from the wall, showed her the loops again and then pulled it undone.

"You try it," he said.

Jessica tried without any success. The halter simply fell apart. She was laughing happily.

"There's a trick to it," she said.

"It isn't a trick at all." Jim was laughing too.

Jessica held out her hand:

"Let me have another go."

Jim told her how to do it, step by step, still unaware that Curly was watching everything through the window. Jessica performed each movement as she was told, but it did not work.

"Wrong!" Jim exclaimed. "What happened?"

"I don't know," she said and they were laughing together so gaily that neither of them heard the soft sound of a horse's hooves in the dust of the yard.

Harrison rode into the stables on his toey dappledgrey. The grey was sweating, and Harrison looked as if he had been riding hard. Eyeing the scene in Kip's stall with intense disapproval, he swung off his horse.

"Get about your business, Jessica," he said abruptly.

"And you," he turned to Jim, "cool off this horse and stable him."

Jim felt as if he were doomed always to be made to look foolish and inferior. He took the reins and led the horse out, but the big dappled-grey half pulled back as they rounded the corner of the building. Jim stopped in his tracks, looking sharply to see what had startled the horse. Slowly a smile spread over his face. For there on a water-barrel sat Curly, absorbed in his effort to make an instant halter.

Curly looked up suddenly, aware that he was being watched: he was caught. He looked silly, and he knew it.

"It's called the Tom Fool Knot," Jim grinned, thinking: "At least that's one to me!"

Curly's mouth dropped open.

Jim leant over and patted him on the shoulder:

"You're getting the hang of it. I'll be back later to check on your work." Half-laughing, he knew it was two to him now.

Some time later, however, while still working on the grey, Jim saw Jessica out of the corner of his eye leading Kip across the yard, talking to her father. Though he could not hear what they were saying, Jessica did not look pleased—nor did Harrison.

Harrison spoke angrily:

"I've told you before not to bother the stockmen."

"No one was bothering anyone," Jessica retorted. "I only wanted to saddle Kip and ride out to see a brood mare that's foaling—she'll need help."

"I didn't raise my daughter to be a midwife to a herd of horses. The men can handle that," Harrison said.

Jessica spoke firmly:

"I can do it better."

Her father looked stern.

"It's not a fit occupation for a lady."

"A lady!"

"Yes, lady," Harrison growled. "Has the word become old fashioned?"

"It's become an excuse to keep women under

control," Jessica retorted.

"Please spare me your aunt's new-fangled notions." Harrison's voice was cold. "You should be thinking of marriage and children."

"The well-known cattle breeder has a breeding programme for his daughter as well!" Jessica was partly laughing, mainly sarcastic.

By this time Harrison had become really angry.

"You keep a civil tongue in your head, girl," he said. "I don't know where you get this rudeness from."

Jessica mounted her horse:

"I'm my father's daughter, aren't I?"

Harrison did not reply. His eyes narrowed as he watched her ride away.

The barracks was a long, low building, rather dark, Jim thought, probably dark even in daytime. When he went in with his swag and saddle that evening, there did not seem to be many lanterns to light it. But in the fireplace a good blaze roared against the cold of the autumn night. Apart from the area just in front of the fire, the hut was divided into eight open cubicles in each of which was a bunk and a chest of drawers.

Jim looked around the long, dark hut with its flickering shadows thrown up by the fire and the lanterns. A small group of men, including both Curly and Moss, was playing cards; away from them, an older man was busy carving a small piece of wood with his penknife. Not one of them took any notice of him.

Jim walked a step or two further in, cleared his throat, and asked:

"Which bunk is mine?"

Curly did not even look up from his fistful of cards.

"Any that does not buck you off," he said and there was general laughter.

Finally the older man came to Jim's rescue:

"That one's empty, son," and he pointed to one furthest from the fire. "It's yours if you want it. You can keep your saddle in the tack room."

"Yair." Curly still had not raised his head. "You can stop there yourself, if you like."

The older man spoke quietly:

"Grow up, Curly."

Curly grunted:

"Go to hell, Frew, old man!"

Slowly Frew closed the small blade of his knife, snapping open the larger blade with his thumb. He looked hard at Curly before slicing firmly into the piece of wood that he was carving. His voice was low and even:

"Watch your tongue, boy, while you've still got one."

Though Curly glared, he remained silent. It was obvious that Frew meant what he said. The card game continued.

Jim started to unpack his gear, sensing the hostility towards him but thinking with half his mind: "I'll bloody well teach them!" The other half of his mind—and all his body—was filled with a longing for the mountains. He had been right: the scent of the mountain eucalypts would only rarely be borne down here on the evening breeze, nor would he ever sense that strange silence that had so often pervaded the mountain hut—a whispering silence, of snow falling into snow, flecking the slab walls, weighing down the shingle roof.

As he hung up his gear, he heard the distant threnody of a plover. Plovers called at night in the mountains too; they mourned all the sadness of death—the haunting sadness of the world and yet its glory.

The card game went on, the men's voices murmuring above the crackling of the fire.

As the men argued about the hands that were dealt, good hands and bad, fair cards or lousy, they exchanged gossip on matters of far greater interest. Curly announced that Kane had said they were starting the high country muster in a day or two. A tall man who Jim had not seen before mumbled that he had heard that it would be at the end of the week. Moss muttered that Kane thought there might be an early winter.

"I thought Harrison controlled the seasons," Curly

interrupted.

There was a slapping of cards on the table, and mutters of "I'll take two", or "dealer takes three", and Jim's mind began to fill with pictures of a mountain muster, fill with the song of the Snowy River as it bubbled beneath glittering ice and played around organ-pipe icicles that hung from the pimelia bushes along the banks. His mind began to fill too with a vision of great granite tors, rearing above snowgrass slopes and the last, high, weird-limbed snow gums. And then he saw, almost as the cause of his being forced to be far from his beloved mountains, that magnificent, wild stallion rearing against the moonlight.

Interrupting these thoughts came the raised voice of one of the stockmen:

"They'll hold the muster back till Clancy gets here."

"Your trick," said Curly, then: "Is Clancy really as good a rider as he's cracked up to be?"

The stockman, carefully studying his hand, pulled his beard reflectively.

"I tell you, Clancy's no rider—he's a horseman!" he said. "I'll look!"

"I'll look, too." Moss announced.

Curly put down his hand.

"Two ladies."

"Beats me," the stockman sighed, but Moss was excited.

"I've got a full house," he said.

Curly just looked at him.

"Jeez, you're stupid."

Moss was puzzled.

"Why, Curly?" he said. "This is the second hand I've won."

When Curly ignored Moss and asked, instead, what was really so special about Clancy, Jim knew that Curly was a bad loser and suspected that he believed himself to be the best rider on the station.

The bearded stockman sighed in exasperation and answered him:

"I told you, he's a horseman."

Suddenly Frew spoke up:

"More than that. He's a magician, a genius."

Jim could contain himself no longer.

"I've met Clancy," he said. Young and inexperienced, Jim hoped this might help him gain some respect amongst the other men but instead the eyes that turned to him were openly hostile. He felt his face going red, and faltered: "When I was young: my father and he were mates."

"Gawd strewth!" Curly hooted with laughter. "Mates! Codswallop!"

The others, all except Frew, laughed their disbelief. Curly shook his head, still cackling.

Jim tried to ignore them. Angry with them, and himself, he took his saddle outside to the tack room, found a spare rack on which to put it, covered it with his saddle cloth, and carefully hung his bridle on the hook beneath. He tried quite fiercely not to let the loneliness and the mocking laughter—and Harrison's obvious dislike—really hurt him.

He knew he would have to stick it out, and make enough money to pay off his debts, before he could earn the right to return home to the mountains. He was thankful for the times his father had taken him to picnic races, where he had learnt something about Curly's type, and he was thankful for the boxing lessons his father had given him . . . who knows, they might yet come in useful. Everything seemed to be lost except the intangible gifts from his parents, and Andy, that grand little horse Spur had presented to him.

Jim remembered how he had taken Andy out in the mountains before leaving Spur's place. In memory, he felt the smooth action, as they had cantered along the soft snowgrass plains and ridges. They had ridden across boulder-filled streams, and Andy had never faltered. Jim had helped one of those mountain men who had been at his father's funeral to muster his cattle, and that small horse had been absolutely sure-footed down a steep rough slope.

He was a real mountain horse, that Andy.

It was early morning, and Jim had finished his customary tasks of filling the woodbox and mucking out the stalls. He noticed there was an unusual amount of activity near the yards. It seemed to him that all the station hands had found themselves jobs, however unnecessary, that kept them in sight of the road.

Joining in the game was probably in order, he decided, as long as he remained inconspicuous. He carried more wood up to the house. As he stacked it by the box, he saw Harrison come out with Kane on to the verandah and look towards the yards.

"What in God's name are they all doing?" Harrison asked Kane. "Is this some kind of a union meeting?"

Kane laughed.

"They've heard that Clancy is coming . . . It's not often that anyone gets to see a legend."

Jim, who really could only just remember Clancy from many years ago, had guessed the reason for the "union meeting" all along. Now he caught sight of a horseman followed by a packhorse, a long way down the track. A murmur spread through the station hands as all eyes watched the two horses approach against a backdrop of blue mountains, making their way across rolling green paddocks, sometimes obscured by the great spreading red gums when the track to the homestead twisted between trees.

"Here he comes." The whisper passed from man to man, but Jim stood in silence, simply watching.

As the horseman came closer, he became more and more impressive. First of all the waiting men could see that the horse was a showy brown. The early sunlight glinted off his hide as he pranced along. Light shone on stirrup irons and bridle buckles, flashed on the buckles on the rider's quart pot and saddle pouch.

The rider sat his horse gracefully, relaxed, simply a part of the rhythm. Soon his neat clothing could be made out . . . his hat with just a wide enough brim to show that

Clancy of the Overflow came from further north, a waistcoat of colours just short of being flash, and moleskin pants that fitted perfectly on his slim, neat figure. His boots were polished, as was his saddle. Even the black packhorse moved well, holding its head jauntily.

If Spur had seen Clancy on this occasion, it might have been difficult for the old miner—after putting up with his mocking and insults—to have recognised this carefully created image of Clancy the legend. Each dancing step of that beautiful brown horse, as it carried Clancy closer to the yards, seemed designed to show off the highest qualities of both the man and his horse.

At last they arrived at the yards and Clancy was acknowledging greetings from the assembled stockmen. Politely he nodded to them, for they were all strangers, but at the same time he seemed to be looking around for someone—because he had heard on the "bush telegraph", since leaving Spur's place, that young Jim Craig was working for Harrison.

Then Jim, standing shyly apart from the others, saw Clancy looking straight at him, found his eyes caught and held as the magnificent horseman rode up to him, dismounted, and shook hands.

"Jim Craig, isn't it?" Clancy said. "Been a long time."

Jim was almost unable to speak, but managed to stammer:

"Yes sir." He took the reins which Clancy handed to him. "I'll see to your horses?"

Clancy waved a hand at the packhorse:

"Watch that one," he said. "He's a hog for water."

Jim began to lead the two horses away. Clancy waited till he had gone a few steps, and then raised his voice, speaking loud enough for all the stockmen to hear:

"Oh Jim!" He paused while Jim stopped and turned round. "I was real sorry to hear about your father. He was a good mate."

Jim gazed at the horseman in silent gratitude.

"Thank you," he said finally, in that moment

realising how justified was the immense pride he had always felt in his father.

Clancy moved off towards the homestead verandah, well aware of the expression of envy on Curly's face and delighted by the gladness now apparent in Jim's whole bearing as he took the horses off to the stables.

Chapter Five

"I Have No Brother"

Now that Clancy had arrived, the autumn muster in the mountains would be starting any day.

That afternoon Paterson also arrived. Jim saw Harrison lead him and Clancy down to the yard where they could take a look at the beautiful young colt from old Regret before the light faded. The three men leant on the yard rails, watching the young animal's lithe movements, appraising his upthrown head with its "look of eagles".

Jim, from much further away, saw that head silhouetted against the sunset and felt a stab of—was it almost fear, or recognition, or simply acknowledgement of young, vital perfection? The colt's head against the sunset clouds, that stallion's head against the moon: Jim stood momentarily disturbed by some ghost from the past or some vision of the future which simply did not touch the three men, as each stood with one foot on the lower rail, their arms across the top rail.

Everyone at the barracks knew that quite an occasion was being made of dinner at the homestead that night. All afternoon Mrs Bailey had kept Jim busy fetching wood for her stove and buckets of water, but she also sometimes gave him a big wedge of sponge cake heaped with cream, or some delicious grapes.

As dinner hour arrived, Harrison was in a jovial humour. He and Paterson were both dressed in black dinner jackets and gleaming white shirts. Clancy's buff-coloured suit was neat, well cut, and certainly did not look as if it had come out of a packsaddle bag.

Jessica joined them at the dinner table, together with Harrison's widowed sister-in-law, Rosemary Hume, who managed his household for him. Both the older woman and the girl were very elegantly dressed.

Harrison was explaining to Paterson how he, born an east coast American, came to be an Australian grazier:

"They said to me: go west, young man. Well I did . . . ten thousand miles further than they intended." He laughed, pleased with his own witty remark. "And I found gold after all." He noticed Paterson's questioning expression, and he waved his hand to encompass all his land, out in the darkness beyond the homestead walls. "In beef cattle," he explained. "We made more selling meat to the miners than they ever dug from their claims. Didn't we, Clancy?"

Clancy smiled as he remembered:

"Well, I was the drover. You sold them." He turned to the others round the table: "He was known round the diggings as the Californian horse trader."

Harrison, smiling, got up and walked to the sideboard. Clancy addressed himself to Rosemary:

"That's the finest trifle I have ever eaten, Mrs Hume."

"It's more than a trifle, Clancy. It's a *charlotte russe*."

Harrison, coming back with a port decanter in his hand, set it on the table.

"*Charlotte russe*," he grunted. Looking first to Clancy, on his left hand side, and then to Paterson, on his right, he commented: "My dear sister-in-law occasionally bestows on us simple bush people the fruits of her learning."

Both Paterson and Clancy were amused. Paterson, at least, was aware that Harrison and his dead wife's sister took a delight in their verbal sparring, and that the honours had probably been fairly evenly divided over the years. Except, he suspected, that Rosemary had more often won with regard to Jessica's education and upbringing.

Rosemary now made quite a point of this.

"It's as well that I did, Harrison," she said firmly, "or Jessica would have been brought up with the kangaroos, and we'd be dining in a bark hut tonight."

Harrison's smile at his guests was benign.

"Rosemary does not always appreciate the sacrifices that have to be made to build a property like this." He passed the port to Clancy, who in turn passed it across the table to Paterson, where, after Harrison had poured himself a glass, the decanter finally remained.

Rosemary, with only the faintest twinkle in her eye, asked Paterson to pass it to her.

"Oh, I'm sorry. I . . ." Paterson diplomatically stopped himself from saying anything further, and passed the decanter to her. He also had a twinkle in his eye as she poured out the port.

"There is no reason why women should not enjoy the same privileges as men," she said softly.

Harrison rolled his eyes up into his eyebrows.

"Now Rosemary . . . none of your speeches . . ."

Jessica picked up the decanter and filled her own glass, continuing her aunt's speech, though giving a slightly different twist to it:

"Aunt Rosemary is quite right . . . Well, women should have the right to do anything they are capable of doing."

"What! Drink their port! If they have the head for it!" Harrison scoffed, and turned to Paterson. "Do you hear that! Even my own daughter is becoming infected with this nonsense."

"Who's talking nonsense?" Rosemary asked. "Your own daughter, as you well know, has a good mind. She

49

also has a way with horses and an eye for cattle, a knowledge and understanding of stock breeding. Why shouldn't she develop those gifts? Do you wish to condemn her to a life of domestic dullness?"

"God in heaven!" Harrison exclaimed and, looking at Jessica, said:

"You should be in a ladies' college, and not in the stables."

Paterson was smiling:

"Whatever the complexities of the argument, Mrs Hume," he said, "you are certainly proof that the legal profession has been denied the services of a great advocate." He raised his glass to her.

"Bah!" Harrison was not altogether amused. "We'll never have women lawyers!"

Clancy refilled his glass. Then, never at a loss, he raised it to both the women, sweeping it from Jessica back to Rosemary, whom he now toasted:

"That such sweet libation should have fathered . . . sorry, Mrs Hume . . . *mothered* such a disputation."

Clancy succeeded in softening Harrison's hostility to the women and in getting him to join in the laughter around the table. Once he had them all laughing, the drover added:

"This excellent port is a far cry from the black rum we used to drink on the track."

Harrison raised his glass:

"Well, here's to those long ago days on the cattle roads."

Clancy responded:

"Well, for me, they're not long gone, so here's to their future."

"Ah, but there's no long-term future there, Clancy," Harrison said.

"I wouldn't swap the sunlit plains for all the tea in China." Clancy held up his glass to eye level and gazed into it as though he were looking into the future in that deep-red wine. "They are, indeed, a vision splendid."

Jessica's eyes were wide open with surprise:

"Clancy, how romantic!" she cried delightedly, but Clancy was smiling to himself at his theft of Spur's romantic phrase.

Harrison saw no romance in the subject and exclaimed:

"Man, your brain's gone soft. That's a vision of what's past. All that's gone now there's the railway through and good hard roads being made. We'll soon be shipping refrigerated beef to the markets of England and Europe. That's where the future lies, Clancy."

"Well," Clancy said, shaking his head sadly, "you were always a long way ahead of the old squatters. Which is why, I suppose, there are very few of them left."

Harrison interrupted:

"They tore the guts out of the country."

Clancy was suddenly angry:

"*They* tore the guts out of the country?"

They argued back and forth for a while as Harrison outlined his dream of Australia becoming one of the great food producing countries of the world.

Clancy asked him, a note of cynicism creeping into his voice:

"So you've got it all under control?"

"Yes, I have," Harrison answered. "All except the Snowy Mountains. If I had the capital, I'd run fences up there, cut the big timber, and turn it into the best summer grazing in the country."

"Praise be for the lack of capital," Clancy declared, draining his glass and seeing, in memory, the tall straight trunks not far from Spur's hut.

The argument was becoming a little heated now, so Paterson, the country-bred city lawyer, stepped in:

"Ladies and gentlemen, may I propose a toast. To our two romantics!"

"Eh?" Harrison was caught off balance.

Turning to Clancy, Paterson explained, holding his glass high:

"To one who sees what is!" Then, turning to Harrison: "And to one who sees what can be! Lord grant that the two are compatible . . . and that the Snowy and the Murray continue to flow."

Rosemary and Jessica picked up their glasses quickly. Clancy and Harrison exchanged charged, thoughtful glances, but they smiled at each other and Clancy said:

"Will we charge our glasses and drink to the last part of Barty's toast?"

Harrison did not answer, but he raised his glass, and they all drank.

In that moment of silence, after drinking the toast, as Barty Paterson's words were sinking in, still making ripples, the door opened. Jim stood there with a huge armful of logs.

To Jim the scene was almost unbelievable. His mother had owned some tablecloths, gradually kept, as the years went by, for special occasions. She had had a few pieces of good china—but this shining damask cloth reaching to the floor, the silver and glass glistening on its snow-white surface, the soft, warm light of the lamps, the glow of the red wine in the decanter, the shimmer of the cut glass—this was all quite beyond his imaginings.

His mother had left books which he had read, books that gave some idea of grand dinner parties in Walter Scott's castles in Scotland, but this, after all, was just a homestead in Australian cattle country. Then he realised that he had walked into an awkward silence—a silence which he had not caused.

"Er . . . Mrs Bailey said to bring some firewood," he said.

Clancy's eyes twinkled—what was Mrs Bailey up to? He said:

"Evening, Jim," and Paterson said:

"Hullo there, Jim."

Jessica smiled, her voice joining in too:

"Good evening, Jim."

Harrison looked surprised and not exactly pleased. Everyone seemed to know his wood-and-water joey.

"Well," he growled, "we all seem to be introduced.

Dump the logs." It was an order, but Rosemary intervened.

"Not all of us, Harrison." And she turned to Jim: "I'm Mrs Hume." She took no notice of Harrison's glare.

Jim felt stiff and nervous, but managed to say:

"How do you do, Mrs Hume." Having put down his logs, he was starting to make his escape when Clancy said:

"Jim, we were talking of taming the Snowy River country. You know it better than any of us. What do you think?"

There was another silence, in which the far-away call of the plover came up through the dark of the night, and Jim saw, in his imagination, the Ramshead tors, above Groggin Gap, as he had so often seen them—grey granite tors rising above snowgrass, and above the white and silver of snow daisies—and he saw it with all his desperate love.

He knew he had to say something, and yet he knew that it was not his place to tell the man who had created so perfect a station property that no one should try to rule the mountains, not their sphagnum bogs nor their streams. How could they, indeed, rule the blizzards and great falls of snow?

"I think you might sooner hold back the tide than tame the mountains," he said, "or control the melting of the snow." Then, feeling it was time to go, in more ways than one, he asked to be excused, and went out, closing the door and heaving a sigh of relief.

"That boy has quality about him," Paterson declared, pleased with the lad he had introduced to Harrison. He was unprepared for Harrison's venomous remark:

"Yeah, the mongrel quality of the mountain people!"

Jessica looked angry and upset, and Rosemary seemed more anxious than Harrison's outburst warranted.

But Clancy merely had a mischievous twinkle in his eye:

"Does your brother share that quality?"

"I have no brother," Harrison said, his face cold and

strained. "Excuse me. We've got an early start in the morning." So saying, he left the table and went out the door.

Clancy had got more than he bargained for. He sat, a sad smile barely playing around his lips, turning the glass in his hands by its slim stem. While Jessica—startled, frowning—looked questioningly at her aunt, Paterson, the creator of ballads, the dreamer of dreams, watched Clancy with profound interest.

But Rosemary was visibly distressed, as though some ghost from the past had suddenly touched her. Then a horse's high neigh to the night, from very close by, sent an uncontrollable shudder through her.

Chapter Six

SHARED SECRET

Back in the barracks, when Mrs Bailey had finally let him off, Jim found that there was much activity. Men were greasing saddles, bridles and whips, checking girths, stirrup leathers, breastplates and cruppers. Not one buckle must give, not one strap must break. Hobbles were packed into saddlebags, their straps well greased. Oilskins were being rolled tightly, valises packed and folded. Amongst it all, a small wiry stockman was reading loudly from the Bible.

Curly, still envious of Jim for his apparent friendship with Clancy, looked at Jim's saddle and made a caustic remark about the last time he'd seen a saddle like that — in a circus, with a monkey riding in it.

Jim grinned at him. He felt much more confident since Clancy had singled him out and, anyway, tomorrow they were going off to the mountains which he knew so well — so much better than the others did.

"Where's your rope, Curly?" he mocked, picking up a rope and looping it to make a Tom Fool Knot, then letting it fall apart. The sneering remark which Curly was about to make died on his lips.

The door was shoved open suddenly, and Kane came in. The general talk ceased. Kane was a man who commanded respect.

"We're leaving at sunrise," he said, "and we'll eat at Perry's house."

Frew gave a deep chuckle. Perhaps he was the only one who dared.

"The beef Harrison'll be eating at old Perry's will be his own — only he won't know it," he said.

A roar of laughter shook the shingle roof, and then quietened. Kane's expression did not invite any more remarks of that kind.

Jim was very excited. The muster itself would be great and, as well as going back to the mountains, he would be involved in an important job. He might be starting to earn the right to return to his home.

"Anything special we've got to take?" he asked.

Kane looked at Jim's gear, all neatly laid out on his bed.

"There's been a change of plan," he said. "You won't be going on this muster, Jim."

Jim could barely believe his ears. Then he heard Curly's cackle of laughter, and knew he must have heard right. He had to fight with himself not to look like a miserably disappointed child.

"Harrison probably got a look at that alpine mule of yours," Curly said, and guffawed loudly again.

Jim's back was up and he spoke angrily:

"He's a mountain horse and he knows that country even better 'n I do."

Kane moved a little closer to him as he said:

"I don't make the orders, but when I give them, that's the end of it." Looking at Curly coldly, he added: "Anyone not ready to go at dawn gets his backside kicked."

"Amen," the short stockman said, closing his Bible with a bang.

Kane had seen Jim on his horse, bringing in a few steers, and knew that both horse and boy were well up to the job. But Harrison had expressly given that order. Jim was not to go.

Jim was waiting for him outside the barracks.

"Mr Kane," he said, "why? Why me?"

Kane did not answer straight away.

"I think I know," Jim said slowly.

Kane patted him on the shoulder, and said:

"You'll get your chance, Jim." That was all. He went off to his own house leaving Jim to go back into the barracks to face Curly's derision, and Moss always backing Curly up.

Later Frew quietened the two of them, growling at them to bloody well let a man get some sleep. But the bitterest time was still to come for Jim.

Before sun-up, the men and horses started assembling at the yards. The first rays of light were fanning up in shafts between early clouds; the air was cold, and the breath of men and horses hung in little ghosts of fog before dissolving away. Kane kept Jim busy at the yards, hoping that if the boy were about, perhaps Harrison might change his mind again.

Disconsolately, feeling almost shamed, Jim moved about the yard, holding Kane's horse for him, helping with packhorses. He saw the homestead, a block of darkness except for the few lighted windows. He saw the door open, saw Jessica come out with Harrison, saw Harrison's arm around her. As he saw Jessica stand on tiptoe to kiss her father goodbye, Jim did not know that Harrison was firmly refusing her request to be allowed to go on the muster next time.

Jim watched Harrison walk swiftly towards the white gate, saw him push it shut behind him, and start towards the yards. Then he saw Clancy, on his showy brown, come from another direction.

Harrison mounted his dappled-grey, not throwing a word or even a look in Jim's direction. It was Clancy who saw Jim standing there, not mounted, Clancy who said:

"That boy knows the country better than any of us. He should be coming." But he said no more when he saw

Harrison looking straight ahead, the set line of his mouth. It was Harrison's cattle that they were going to muster, and it was not Clancy's place to say who should be on the job. He gave Jim a friendly nod as they rode by.

There were white Leghorn hens scattering everywhere in front of the mob of horsemen and their packhorses. Curly was far enough in the rear for him to feel certain that Clancy would not hear his parting shot at Jim.

"Don't forget to feed the chooks, Bandicoot." And he grinned maliciously. Frew went through the gate last, giving Jim a salute.

Jim, forlornly watching the party ride off to muster in his own mountains, was aware of Jessica, also left behind. Still standing on the verandah, she waved.

The sun rose: he felt its warmth on the side of his face. Then he heard his own little horse neigh, and, instead of getting straight to work in the empty stables, he went to give him some hay. Andy, almost as sensitive to Jim's moods as a dog might be, now rubbed his head against his master, bunting gently.

"We'll make out, Andy," Jim said, and stayed for a while, rubbing his ears and talking to him.

But there were jobs to be done — one of them being to feed and water the colt. So he got some food for the prize horse before going on with his other duties around the homestead. By mid-afternoon he was almost cheerful as he started to fill the kitchen woodbox for the second time and could hear emerging from one of the inner rooms of the house the sound of a piano being played rather inefficiently.

Mrs Bailey opened the door to offer him a buttered slice of brownie and said:

"When the woodbox is full, Jim, you could be a good lad and carry the afternoon tea tray up to the front room for me, to save my legs."

Jim looked at his boots and his work-calloused hands, but there was no possibility of refusing her, not with another slice of brownie sitting waiting for him. He cut more wood, split some kindling, stacked up the box, and, carefully brushing his boots on the mat, walked in.

"Good boy," Mrs Bailey smiled, giving him the other piece of her brownie to eat while she made the tea. Then she handed him a laden tray, and pushed him through the door with it, across a verandah and along a corridor to the "second door on the right".

The sound of the piano stopped, and Jim heard Mrs Hume's voice say:

"Really Jessica, you're attacking that piece with all the sensitivity of a road mender. Let's begin again. This time, 'con amore'."

Jim set down the tray on a table by the door and knocked. When he heard Rosemary Hume call out to come in, he opened the door and picked up the tray, desperately concentrating on not spilling the milk or letting the scones slide off their plate.

"Excuse me," he said. "Mrs Bailey said I should bring this, to save her legs."

"Hello... Whoops!" said Jessica, seeing at a glance that the tray was in peril, and taking it from him quickly.

Rosemary Hume sighed with relief as the tray was safely retrieved.

"Hello, Jim," she said. "You've saved Jessica having to play her piece of music again. Stay and have tea with us."

Jim had already seen, in one bemused glance, the chintz chair-covers and the velvet curtains; he had felt the soft carpet underfoot and had also noticed Jessica's skirt and blouse, and her beautiful lace jabot.

"No, I couldn't, Mrs Hume," he said, trying not to shuffle his feet.

"Nonsense," she said. "Male company will be a pleasant relief in this hot-house of female emotions." Jim felt even more bemused because he hardly knew what she meant. But he heard Jessica say:

"Go on."

Her aunt told Jessica to pour the tea, while she went for another cup.

Feeling awkward, Jim looked round for something on

which he could sit without making it dirty, and chose the piano stool. As Rosemary Hume left the room, Jessica poured two cups of tea and handed Jim one. It was a small, floral cup on a fragile-looking saucer. Jim's rather dirty hand shook and the teaspoon rattled, seeming to make a great noise in the silence that had suddenly seized the two of them.

Jessica tried to start some conversation:

"We're both feeling sorry for ourselves today, missing out on the muster."

Jim just nodded, and then, as though thinking aloud, said:

"Seems like they're trying to make a butler out of me."

Jessica smiled broadly.

"Well," she said, "they're trying to make a lady out of me."

Jim, his mind still on his own troubles, barely heard her remark, and went on talking as if she had not said anything.

"They won't have no luck," he said.

Jessica flew up.

"Thank you *very* much," she blazed, as a daughter of Harrison's might be expected to blaze.

Jim looked startled, realising what he had said.

"Hang on, that's not what I meant. I was meaning . . ."

"They won't make a gentleman out of you either." Jessica had the last word.

Flushing bright red, unaware of what he was doing, Jim started to play the first few bars of a hymn that had been a favourite of his mother's.

"Can you play?" Jessica asked.

"My mother was starting to teach me, before she died . . ." He went on playing, almost speaking to himself:

"She taught me . . . so . . . much . . ."

"How long ago did she die?" Jessica asked.

"Three years ago."

"Do you miss her?" Jessica had moved closer to the piano.

"Yes... Yes, I do miss her."

"I never knew my mother."

Jim stopped playing. This was something different. The girl would have been too young to feel a real sense of loss, but all the same, Jim found it difficult to imagine a baby being brought up without its mother. He could remember going out into the bush in front of his mother's saddle, travelling miles and miles through the great forests, could remember the stories she used to read him, all the fun, the care. So many memories — the wanderings over "the tops" as he grew older, collecting the wildflowers they picked and pressed, the specimens they sent to the great botanist, Baron von Mueller, for identification.

"I'm sorry," he said. "She would have been pretty — like you."

Jessica was moved by the way in which he said it. Their eyes met and held momentarily, as though each were a magnet for the other — Jim's clear blue, and Jessica's purple-blue, almost violet. But then Jim looked away, trying to break the magnetic force, leaving Jessica confused, still looking at him.

Jim was confused, too. What was he doing, in Harrison's sitting-room, telling his daughter that she was pretty? He gulped down his tea and stood up as though propelled from behind.

"Thank you for the tea... Miss Jessica. I'd better finish my jobs."

He went out quickly, passing Mrs Hume in the corridor and thanking her for the tea. Smiling over her shoulder at him as she went in the door, her smile became a little thoughtful when she heard Jessica playing the piano, saw the expression on her face. But she tried to persuade herself that they were just two children, both sadly disappointed at being left out of the autumn muster on "the tops".

The autumn evening was closing in. Magpies were carolling high in the silver-blue and the pale rose of the sky above Harrison's softly rolling, green paddocks, above his peacefully grazing Hereford cattle. The cherry red of the Herefords looked darker, now the sunlight had gone, and their white faces and legs, the white stripe down their necks and backs, looked more intensely white. Here and there, a wide, raking pair of horns reflected the sky's light.

Jim, his expression wan, stood gazing out at the scene. His whole self was longing to be in the mountains. He, who belonged there, had been left behind. Then there came into his mind the echo of that old mountain man's voice: "Earn the right to live up here like your father did."

He shook himself, and turned towards the feed room, to mix up a feed for the colt — and something for Andy. For a few moments more, he watched the magpies zooming up into bright light, glittering there in the sky, and then he went in and began measuring out chaff and bran, mixing them together.

He went to Andy first.

"I'll get time to ride you tomorrow, boy," he whispered, determined to ride around and see the cattle in some paddocks into which he had not yet been. He buried his face in Andy's warm neck and mane, the company of his horse briefly dispelling his loneliness. Then he picked up the colt's bucket and strode off.

It was while he was giving the colt his bran mash, patting him, stroking him, talking to him, that Jessica came to the yards. The colt felt her presence before Jim did, and when the finely-bred, black head came up to inspect the second visitor, Jim looked up, surprised.

"He's lovely, isn't he?" Jessica said.

Jim's hand was resting on the young horse's neck.

"Truly beautiful," he said, and their pleasure in the colt felt like some sort of bond between them. After a while Jim added:

"There's not a mean bone in his whole body."

"Curly will find one," said Jessica shortly.

"What's he got to do with it?" Jim sounded surprised.

"He does all the horse breaking here."

"Curly! That oaf would ruin an animal like this." The colt, as though hearing the agitation in Jim's voice, nuzzled him.

Jessica was half-laughing, half-startled by his vehemence.

"You've got to be firm with a young horse," she said.

"Firm," Jim agreed, "but not cruel. You work with the horse, not against him. Me and my dad have been breaking in horses for years."

He rubbed his face against the colt's neck, realising with a sweep of sorrow that he would not be breaking in any more horses with his father.

"This is not just a brumby," Jessica said.

"It's no different," Jim told her. "And there are thoroughbreds among the brumbies. They've not been fed so well, that's about all."

"Are you saying you could break in this horse?" she asked.

"Yes, I could."

"Well?" Jessica made a long drawn-out question of the word.

"What about your father?" Jim asked.

To Jim, she did not seem to have made a very strange suggestion. He had broken in so many horses since his father first recognised how quickly they trusted him.

"He'll be away for more than a week. If the job's done before he gets back, what can he say? I'd hate to see Curly get his hands on this one."

Jessica was gaining confidence in her idea, especially when she saw that Jim did not consider it foolish at all. She saw, in fact, that Jim thought of horse breaking as his real job.

Jim stood, warmed by the last rays of the sun, almost blinded by a sunshaft, though he could still see the colt's mane and hair blazing with light. He was lost in his own thoughts, and unaware that his face was burnished copper in the sunset, for Jessica alone to see.

The colt bunted him gently. Jim knew that the young horse had trusted him since that day in the station yard. He heard Jessica saying:

"He'll do anything for you, Jim, anything you want to teach him," and he knew that this was so.

Still deep in thought, he said:

"From old Regret . . . Somewhere, a long time ago, I've heard that name." He stood back a little from the colt, seeing him outlined by the sunset, and a faint feeling of recognition, as though something were stirring in his memory, came over him. He shivered.

"Goose walk over your grave?" Jessica's eyes were laughing at him.

"He reminds me of something," Jim said. "Just something I can't quite place." After a moment, he added:

"He really is the most beautiful horse I've ever seen." He smiled at Jessica — and he knew he would break in the colt.

He would handle him slowly, quietly, in the time left over from doing all the jobs which Kane expected him to do. He would ride him, eventually, in between riding his own horse, because he must keep Andy in good nick. Then, as he was thinking of Andy, he suddenly knew that he loved that little, wiry mountain horse — the first horse which he had ever entirely owned, and which had seemed to take possession of *him* — better than he would ever love even Harrison's beautiful colt from old Regret.

Though Jim had not actually stated his decision to break in the colt, Jessica knew he would do it, and she appeared at the yards very early next morning, before her aunt could catch her for a music lesson.

Jim had put the colt into the round yard and given him a small feed, which the horse had already finished by the time Jessica arrived. Now it was time to start handling him. Jim had tethered him to "Aunt Sally", as it was called, the post in the middle of the round yard.

"Morning, Jim." Jessica spoke quietly.

Jim looked up, smiling his welcome, glad that she appreciated the need to be quiet, feeling a sudden surge of pleasure in the fact that she had come to watch, come to take part in the breaking in. He began to rub the colt very gently with a towel, very gently rubbing him all over, talking to him, whistling occasionally, almost under his breath, never moving quickly.

Presently he led the colt over to Jessica, where she was watching through the rails.

"May I come in quietly?" she asked. "He's used to being handled by a woman: that's why Father let me bring him off the train."

Jim looked at her with a half grin, but nothing more was said about that particular day. Jessica squeezed through the rails, and stood beside him, both of them patting the colt, running their hands over him.

Day after day, in the early morning and in the evening — when all the other jobs were done — Jim was in the round yard, breaking in the colt from old Regret, mouthing him, driving him in long reins, obtaining his obedience, seeking his good performance and rewarding him for it. Enfolded in the pleasant smell of warm, young horse, he and Jessica shared every improvement, every triumph.

In bright, early mornings, or mornings when the autumn mist spangled hair and hide, in evenings of red sunset that gilded their faces, or evenings of misty rain, Jim and Jessica were at the yards. Jim was performing the breaking in, but Jessica was there too, sharing in the slow, steady process, sharing with Jim his concentrated effort, his love for the horse, his pride in it.

After the half hour or more of training was over, and the colt, with only a headstall on, was just moving peacefully round the yard, the two would sit together on the rails, watching him and talking, their faces rose red in the sunset, or gilded by the dawn. Sometimes their bare arms touched, and an electric flash would go through Jim, and he wondered if Jessica felt it too. Then he would tell himself not to be stupid, that these mornings and evenings could not go on once the men came back from the autumn muster.

Jessica talked about the station, about the life she led and loved, about the cattle and the horses, assuming without question, it seemed to Jim, that it would some day be hers. Jim's talk of himself was more guarded, but somehow Jessica learnt how much it had hurt him when the mountain men had told him that he could not live on his own place in the mountains till he had earned the right to do so; she, who had never had to earn anything, also began to appreciate his need to earn money.

They laughed together over Jim's story of the difficulties of once sharing a tutor with the children of a family who lived nearer Jindabyne; they talked together about picnic race meetings, which were almost the only occasions on which either of them had met many other people, though Jessica did have a few stories of going to visit other stations.

Most of all, Jim talked about the mountains — of the brilliant blue lakes below rock crags, the carpets of snow daisies, the pink, white and purple eye-brights. He told her of a field of creamy white gentianella vibrating in a mountain breeze, of the sweet scent of the white-starred heath at evening, of all the flowers that he and his mother had collected and studied. Jessica listened, enthralled, as he evoked the power and the glory of those mountains that held the source of the Snowy River.

Each day grew a little colder. Flocks of gang-gang cockatoos had come down from the mountains, Jim had heard the first robin redbreast's frail song, and a fat grey thrush had woken Jessica once, very early. A light frost one morning silvered the cobwebs that hung between thistles and twigs, making each one into a blazing wheel of life.

Jim thought it would be foolish to mount the colt for the first time in the cold of the early morning, so he decided to arrange his jobs so that he could do it in mid-morning ... mid-morning on a lovely, clear autumn day, with that penetrating, soft light that confers a special magic.

Jessica had managed to get through her music practice and her studies with her aunt quite quickly, and begged to be allowed out. The day was so beautiful, she pleaded, and such weather could not last forever.

Jim was driving the colt in the long reins when she got away from the house and ran down to the yards. He had waited until she got there to ride the colt, wishing to share every excitement with her.

Instead of the breaking in tackle, he put his saddle carefully and slowly on to the young horse's back, and, girthing him up extremely gently, led him round for quite a while. Then he put his foot in the stirrup, and simply *flowed* upwards and into the saddle, talking quietly to the colt all the time, and patting his neck reassuringly. Even so the colt reared, but Jim never shifted his position in the saddle. Only his body moved, absorbing the action of the colt.

Jim knew well that sensation of a young horse being ready to leap in any direction — all directions — the intense feeling of a coiled spring beneath him and between his knees and thighs.

Jessica watched, holding her breath with nervousness, excitement, and then pride, as Jim rode the colt round and round the yard, at a walk, and then at a trot. When Jim thought the colt had had enough, he eased him back to a walk, and rode him straight across to Jessica who stood, dark hair lifting in the breeze, dark blue eyes bright, almost unable to speak with excitement.

Jim dismounted, and she climbed through the rails and they stood together, arms touching with that thrilling contact as they made much of the colt.

That night, after Jim had bedded down the colt in his stable, and fed Andy with lucerne hay, he stood at the stable door looking towards the house. Faintly, on the still evening air, he could hear the piano, this time played with deep feeling, and knew for certain that it was Jessica playing.

The window of the sitting-room glowed in the dusk. She had not pulled the curtains, and the music wove together the autumn sunshine, the frozen cobwebs, the dawns and the sunsets — all the hours that he and Jessica had shared, breaking in the colt, the marvellous hours.

There could only be a few more days, unless Harrison's cattle had strayed the length and breadth of the Snowy Mountains.

That night another frost came to fur-white the fences, the blades of grass, the dried-up thistles, and the coats of the dark red Herefords. The moonlight was cold and clear.

Jim, alone in the barracks, in his sleep heard Andy neigh. But it seemed to be in his dreams, and Jim did not waken. Only the unstabled horses saw, on a distant rise, a stallion standing wild and free against the moonlight, making no sound.

Then he was gone . . . that wild thoroughbred brumby, owning hundreds of miles of unfenced, untamed high mountains and deep ravines, forests and crags, owning and owned by the great winds with which he galloped.

Chapter Seven

THE STALLION AND THE COLT

The time of the musterers' return had to be drawing closer each day. But both Jim and Jessica were shying away from really thinking about the way in which Harrison would—or should—learn about the colt being broken in.

Jessica knew that Jim was doing the job very well. They were both enjoying it greatly—perhaps with a brittle sort of enjoyment because they knew they were experiencing something that had to come to an end. They loved the even sound of the colt's hooves as he trotted round the sandy yard; they both thrilled with pride when Jim rode him, teaching him to canter, to respond to the aids. This was their shared secret.

Since that mid-morning when Jim had first ridden the colt, Mrs Bailey had also been in on the secret, for she had seen them often from the kitchen door. On this particular morning, she had looked out much earlier, knowing they would be out, working the colt. She saw Jim driving him in long reins and Jessica arriving at the yards, noting with a sigh that the girl whom she had helped care for as a baby was no longer a leggy child, but a woman with the same lovely figure which her mother had had. She noted too, with a chill of apprehension, how proudly Jim held himself, how proudly he displayed the colt, how happy Jessica and he were together.

Mrs Bailey saw that Jim was doing very well with the colt, but she was wondering how Harrison was going to be told; how Harrison was going to survive the shock of his colt being broken in, however well, without his permission; how he was going to survive the young ones' friendship. She shrugged her shoulders, thinking how difficult Harrison had made life for others—and himself—and that the scene at the yards looked so happy with the colt moving well and the two working so expertly. Mrs Bailey was just thinking that there had not been all that much happiness over the years, when she saw the colt rear in fright, and knew that something was wrong.

In one flash, Mrs Bailey took in the sight of Jim trying to quieten the colt, then she quickly looked around to see what had frightened him. A sound drew her eyes in the same direction as Jim's. There was something moving swiftly through the big stand of red gums. Suddenly she recognised the sound of the far-away drumming of many hooves.

They were back ... the wild horses, back again, galloping, and with them they brought that seventeen-year-old fear. Something dreadful was going to happen to them, all over again ... More than thirty wild horses, down from the mountains, raced by in broad daylight—this was no dream in the night ...

The colt danced with fear; four stockhorses galloped the fence of their paddock.

Jim saw the brumby herd burst out of the timber and, even at that distance, he recognised the old stallion, recognised Bess galloping with him.

"Bess," he gasped, and then he shouted:

"Bess!"

Suddenly Jim was back on Kelly's Saddle and there was that terrible vision again—a chain breaking, a tree trunk ripping free, crashing, striking; there was his father lying with crushed ribs, his face and head bleeding . . . and there was the gelding with a broken leg.

He had the gate open and was on the startled colt before Jessica's cry rang out:

"Jim! Don't you dare!"

He did not even hear her; he was experiencing the shock of his father's death, seeing Bess vanishing all over again.

Jim had a score to settle. He had to defeat that stallion who was somehow always the bearer of grief; he had to get Bess back. The happiness of the last week was engulfed in the returning tide of all that misery.

Tears running down her cheeks, Jessica clutched the rail of the yard. But Jim was already gone and had not heeded her.

Jim was not really thinking at all: he was just filled with a mad urge to round up the brumbies and catch Bess. As the colt reared, he sat more firmly and urged him into a gallop.

The brumbies were like a frieze of horses, galloping parallel with him, across the peaceful landscape. He must race them, get in front of them, head them. He had the colt well in control: he checked him slightly, and turned him. Ahead was a gate, just a little lower than the post and rail fence. Jim felt a boiling upwards of a wild excitement quite beyond his control.

He had to get Bess, had to defeat that stallion. He collected the colt and urged him by voice, hand and leg up and over the gate.

The colt jumped perfectly—and, Jessica noted with a stab of pride, Jim rode him perfectly. But then she was holding her breath in anguish.

There was another fence, another gate. Jim on the colt only had to clear that gate ahead of the brumbies and he would have them, be able to round them up. The brumby mob went even faster. Jim swung the colt around towards the gate, galloping over rough ground. This gate was higher than the first one.

All that careful training in order to win the colt's

absolute trust . . . now Jim asked too much of him, and put him at the gate.

The colt faltered over a deep rut, but Jim urged him on, fearing the brumby stallion might still be the winner.

The colt was on his wrong leg.

Mrs Bailey had joined Jessica at the yards. Jessica saw the colt's awkward gait, and gave a sob. Then she saw the colt baulk. As Jim, riding bareback and so having no hope of staying on, flew through the air and over the gate, Jessica screamed:

"Jim! Jim!"

He landed straight in the path of the brumby stallion.

As Jim hit the ground, he realised just what he had done. He shook his head, trying to clear away the dazzling stars, and opened his eyes. Horses' legs were racing straight for him. Then the stallion was rearing above: Jim could see his belly and his hooves bearing down on him, striking towards him. As he made a desperate effort to roll away, Jim smelt the strong odour of the horse. Then he heard Jessica screaming.

The horse heard the strange noise. His hooves dropped to the ground. His lip still curling, his nose pinched in, his neck snaking, he took another strike at Jim's rolling body, but without giving more than a glancing blow. Then he gathered his herd together and led them off, a thundering mob of brumbies making back into the timber.

Jim lay there, the world spinning around him, lighting up with bursts of sparks and then going black.

Jim was lying in his bunk, and had not the vaguest idea of how he had got there. A dusty spider's web near the doorway was swaying slightly in a small draught. "All we want's the spider to try, try again," he thought ruefully. "I'm the rottenest bloody fool . . ."

He could hardly bear to think of what he had done. A sweat of horror broke out over him as he thought of that colt, that colt worth a thousand pounds. Aching all over, he tried to sit up, but his head spun and the walls and ceiling of the barracks swayed and swung. Lying back again, he tried to focus on the roof and the spider web, and on the bright stars which had returned when he tried to sit upright.

A little later, half-dozing, he jumped when he heard a knock. Jessica walked in, carrying a tray.

"How's the head?" she asked curtly.

Trying to sit up, the blankets sliding away from his grey flannel, Jim was too embarrassed to speak. But at least, sitting up this time, stars did not dance in front of his eyes any more.

Jessica put the tray down on a rough, hide-covered stool.

"Mrs Bailey told me that this is your favourite . . ."

But all Jim could think of was the horse.

"What happened to the colt?" he interrupted, speaking almost roughly in his desperate need to know.

"We yarded him." Jessica's tone was acid.

"Is he all right?" Jim could barely stop his voice shaking.

Jessica had been badly frightened at the yards, and now anger was close to the surface.

"A bit flighty, but not hurt—luckily."

"There'll be hell to pay when . . . when your father finds out."

"He won't find out. We've all agreed."

Jim's head began to spin again.

"We? Who's we?" he asked, knowing he had really done wrong, and feeling bitter that he had let Jessica down badly . . . let himself down, too.

"Mrs Bailey, Aunt Rosemary, and I," Jessica answered firmly.

Sick and sore, and disgusted with himself, Jim burst out:

"I'm not hiding behind the skirts of a bunch of women."

He had not meant to sound so rude and, hearing himself, he instantly regretted his words.

"Oh," said Jessica, with fury. "I'm so sorry. I must

remember that, next time you try to kill yourself."

Jim felt as if his head would never stop spinning. If only he had resisted that wild feeling that had got into him, that desperate urge to settle the score with the stallion.

But now, with the unreasonableness of the slightly concussed, he felt that he was being bullied by Jessica.

"That's nonsense, Jessica," he said.

She flared up:

"Well, somebody's got to save you from your own thoughtlessness."

This was too much for someone who had landed so hard on his head.

"Don't you Harrisons ever get tired of running other people's lives . . . ?" he shot at her.

She interrupted him:

"You ungrateful . . ."

But he had to finish, even though his vision was blurring, however hard he tried to focus on her:

"Because I'm getting tired of it."

"Well, don't worry." She turned to leave. "That's the last time I'll stand up for the likes of you."

Suddenly realising how rude he had been, Jim called to her:

"Jessica!"

But all she said was:

"You ungrateful . . . fool, Jim."

Jim lay back with a groan. It was not she who had been haunted by the sight of Henry Craig being hit by the falling log, of the mare being taken by that brumby stallion, of the gelding he had had to shoot . . . how could she understand?

From far away, he heard a faint sound of cattle bellowing. As he listened intently, the sound grew louder. Then he heard dogs barking, whips cracking, men shouting at their dogs and whistling—and always the incessant bellowing.

The cobweb swayed faintly in the draught.

The mountain cattle were put into the bottom paddocks,

not right up beside the house, even though the calves would have to be brought up for branding in the yards in a day or so. Each cow, each bullock carried Harrison's brand, the letter H within a diamond.

Harrison watched the last of them go in the gate, watched the men, off their horses, chasing, catching, and pushing the reluctant and bewildered calves through the gate. Red and white cattle spread far out over the paddocks; cows bellowed for their calves, calves bellowed for their mothers and ran about trying to find them. It would be an hour or so before they were all mothered, and quieter.

Harrison, after checking that the gate was doubly fastened, turned for the homestead.

Kane was already in the yards.

"How many short?" Harrison asked him.

"Twenty on that last count."

Sauntering up to Harrison, Curly asked ingratiatingly if he could take Harrison's horse for him.

"Where's the mountain boy?" Harrison snapped.

"Still in his bunk." Curly gave a contemptuous sort of laugh.

Harrison swung off his tired-looking dappled-grey, and strode into the barracks.

Jim had got himself upright and was sitting on his bunk, partly dressed.

"You waiting for breakfast in bed?" Harrison sneered. Then he saw Jim's cut and bruised head. "What happened?"

"I came off the . . . off a horse," Jim stammered.

"Do you think you could get back on?" Harrison was sneering again. "Pick up twenty strays we left on 'the tops'?"

Jim stood up, determined not to show any sign of pain, or to sway with the giddiness that suddenly seized him.

As Harrison walked out, almost brushing against the cobweb near the doorway, he turned and threw a final jibe over his shoulder:

"Twenty, if those mountain men haven't got their grubby hands on them."

Jim, almost as though there were eyes watching him in the barracks, forced himself to move as though he were not aching in his shoulders and back, and in the thigh which had caught that glancing blow from the stallion's hoof. His head had ceased to spin but it, too, was aching.

He took his oilskin off its hook and rolled it tightly, put some spare clothes into his valise and folded an old, thin blanket which he would both use as a saddle cloth and wrap around himself if he were sleeping by a campfire. Then he went out to catch Andy.

Every step hurt but his head was clearing now and he had had enough falls in his life to know that there was no serious damage done and that if he kept moving, the pain would steadily wear off.

He opened the gate, walked into the paddock, and called his horse. Andy came trotting towards him, and life suddenly seemed more promising. Andy gave him his usual bunt in greeting, sniffed at his hurt head, and rubbed against him. Jim put his bruised cheek against the warm neck.

"We're going back to the mountains, Andy," he said. "Just you and I. I guess we can do a good job . . . I guess we'd better."

He was thankful that none of the other men were about as he mounted stiffly. There was no sign of Jessica, and he dared not go and take a quick look at the colt to reassure himself.

As he rode away from the homestead, Jim wondered about the way Harrison had seemed to deliberately set out to make him seem inferior; yet as he and Andy followed the track, along which he had watched Clancy coming, and which was now all churned up by the mob of four hundred cattle, he found himself whistling with pleasure. The mountains lay ahead. Maybe it was just imagination, but he thought he could already smell the mountain ash, their heady eucalyptus scent on the breeze.

The going was soft and only gently rising, and Jim

thought he would try the feel of a canter. He pressed Andy forward. At first he thought he could almost hear his muscles and bones creaking, then the rhythm began to flow into him, the rhythm of Andy's smooth canter and the muffled sound of his hooves. When Jim eased him to a walk again, he was feeling a lot better, even if his head did throb.

Far away, from the direction of the mountains, he heard a calling. Andy pricked his ears, and Jim gazed into the distance. Gradually he saw a whole host of currawongs flying towards him, down from the high country, calling, calling. Soon they were nearly overhead; then they passed, dark birds flying, gliding, quite beyond counting, and still they called.

Jim patted Andy's wither:

"Well," he said, "I bet they're talking of snow, calling out that it's coming. We'll have to be quick, or we may be snow-shoeing out these cattle."

There were miles to go, and hours to ride. Jim and Andy made their way along the trampled cattle track as it wound through peppermint trees, messmate and stringybark. Then, as they rose higher, they began to weave between tall, slim, white ribbon gums. Riding on his own, making very little noise, and with no one ahead to disturb the quiet of the bush, Jim saw birds and animals that would normally have hidden if there had been a whole train of riders and packhorses going single file through the bush.

A dingo crossed the track ahead of him, stood poised for a few seconds, prick-eared, suspicious—yellow dog dingo. A lyrebird scuttled and flopped through the bush into a damp fern gully, its tail hanging as though partly disconnected; several little doves ran along the side of the track, and whirred off into the bush.

Jim swayed gently in time with the long-striding walk of his horse, watching the flickering forest pass, breathing in the strong, somehow biting eucalyptus scent of the peppermint leaves, and the deep, sweet scent of the stringybark blossoms.

In that strange light which glows obliquely from beneath a bank of cloud at evening sat Spur by the window of his hut, wearing his usual mud-stained waistcoat and crumpled trousers, and his ancient, floppy shirt. He held up to the warm, glowing light a velvet picture frame.

There was no mocking expression on his face, no effort to make a sort of crazy joke of life, only sadness, as he gazed at the picture within the velvet frame. Sighing deeply, he closed his eyes.

A sound made him spring up and stump to the door. Out beyond the overhanging limb of a black sallee, Jim was just opening the crookedly hung gate and riding in.

The two men greeted each other warmly, but no questions were asked, no information given until Andy was rubbed down, fed and watered. By then it was almost dark, and they went into the hut.

Jim's hat had hidden the cut on his head, and he reckoned his black eye and bruised cheekbone were not all that noticeable. In the gloom of the hut, by the light of the lantern, neither would probably be seen. Spur busied himself with his stew pot over the fire, and Jim sat himself down in his usual place. Spur put a large bowl of stew in front of him.

Jim grinned.

"It's good to be back," he said. "At least nothing changes up here."

He made no move to eat, but, pausing slightly, he added: "I saw Bess again—with the brumbies. I nearly got her back."

The cheerfulness left Spur and his face darkened.

"I told you not to throw effort after foolishness. Forget her, Jim." Then, changing the subject, Spur asked:

"How are things going down there?"

"Not too good, I'm afraid," Jim said. Then he looked questioningly at Spur:

"I'm working for a fellow called Harrison . . ."

He saw surprise written on Spur's face, and went on:

"He reminds me of someone." As Spur set his mouth firmly shut, Jim added:

"You never told me you had a brother."

"You never asked me," Spur said without showing any emotion.

"Well, I'm asking now."

Spur's voice was friendly, but firm, undoubtedly intending to close the topic:

"You just concern yourself with Jim Craig."

Jim sighed.

"All right—keep it to yourself."

Spur, with his usual adroitness, switched the subject a little:

"Have you seen Jessica?"

"Yes." Jim sounded rather short.

"What's she like?"

"She's a Harrison—a chip off the old block."

Spur snorted, but he also looked a little sad. He said nothing.

Jim looked around the hut with its crazy gadgets and everything leaning this way and that, and then he looked back at Spur, so similar and yet so utterly different from the tall, lithe man with the neatly cropped, thick white hair, the owner of the well-built slab and shingle homestead, the host at that dinner table with the white cloth and glittering glasses.

"I'm getting out after this muster," Jim said.

Spur gave him a quizzical look from under one cocked eyebrow.

"Henry Craig's son quitting?"

"You saying I should stick it out?"

"You can learn more from Harrison than you know."

Jim sat quietly for a few moments, staring into the dark depths of the hut, and then he said:

"I'll be searching for his strays for weeks . . . and I reckon things point to snow coming soon."

"You won't be looking for weeks, if you know where to look."

Surprised, Jim looked hard at Spur, and the old man went on:

"At the first hint of snow, and there's been a

little—higher up—already, every beast on the high country heads towards the Cascades. It's a warm pocket with good forage . . . You could gather them up in a butterfly net there."

"How d' you know?"

Spur put a spoonful of stew in his mouth, and chewed it with obvious relish.

"Well, I don't always eat wallaby, son."

Jim's eyes and face lit up. Putting his nose to his plate and sniffing at it, he began to chuckle.

"Grubby hands," he laughed. "Harrison was right." He took a mouthful himself, biting into the meat, tasting it with care and reverence.

"I'd say prime two-year-old Hereford, fattened on mountain pastures."

Spur grinned.

"Good gracious me! You might make a good cattleman yet."

He rolled his eyes up under his eyebrows, looking like himself again—like a man who had chased the sign of "colour" for years. Jim suddenly wondered if Harrison had some special motive, other than making him prove himself, in sending him out to find the strays. It was not a very comfortable thought.

If Spur observed Jim's bruises in the early morning light, or his stiffness as he saddled his horse and mounted, he said nothing. His face just lit up with pleasure when Jim, sitting with his hand on Andy's neck, remarked:

"No one ever got a better present."

Then he saluted the old man and rode off, heading towards the Cascades.

It was not much past dawn as he rode through the black sallees that surrounded Spur's hut, and climbed upwards among the towering ash. Jim was glad with his whole being to be back in the mountains again—though perhaps thankful that his way did not take him past the hut that had been his old home. There was a wind soughing in the big trees, and when he came out of their shade, he noticed that the sun was very hot. "Something's coming," he told Andy, "but you know that better than I do."

They left the mountain ash for the snow gums: the silver-barked and slim trees, and the great old trunks, gnarled and bent, green and red, orange and silver, knotted and bowed by the weight of the snow and the strength of the streaming wind. Andy stepped over logs and around stumps. Up they climbed until they reached the crest of a ridge.

There, ahead, was the great wall of granite tors and rock ribs, gorges and steep snowgrass faces. A thin frosting of snow lay in shadowed gullies.

Jim reined in, and gazed and gazed, his hand resting on his horse's mane.

Chapter Eight

"As Deceitful as Your Mother"

A pale blue, early morning sky was silvered with mist. One sulphur-crested cockatoo flew across, pewter coloured until it wheeled and caught the light and was suddenly white. Paterson saw it, as he sat on the rails watching the mountain cattle being yarded for drafting and calf branding.

No sound could be heard above the bellowing. Harrison, immaculate as ever, had everything well under command. Watching his purposeful movements, Paterson wondered about the mystery on which Clancy had touched that night, at dinner, before they went mustering. It seemed to have something to do with a brother whom Harrison would not own, something to do with the mountain men.

Paterson felt a little sorry now that he had given that bright and eager boy from the hills an introduction to Harrison. It seemed as if Harrison was giving him a rough time, first refusing to have him on the mountain muster with the other station hands, and then sending him out alone to find the cattle that everyone else had missed . . . if, indeed, they had been missed. Scenting mystery and drama, Paterson thought it would be interesting to have a yarn to Clancy, to see what he could find out.

While his men were drafting one mob, Harrison went around to the yard in which the colt was eating his feed. From his perch on the rails, some distance off, Paterson observed Harrison making a close inspection of the colt, then saw him go striding off towards the homestead. It occurred to Paterson that, even from a distance, Harrison's stride, his whole bearing, looked like that of an angry man, a very angry man.

Paterson had been glad to be able to get himself involved in the work in the yards, but now, he reflected, perhaps it was just as well that he was about to visit a neighbouring station for a few days.

At the homestead, the two older women and Jessica were all working in the kitchen. Rosemary was helping Mrs Bailey with an intricate dessert for that evening's dinner, and Jessica was making herself useful peeling potatoes.

They all knew that Jim had been given the task of mustering the strays and getting them home. Jessica was worried, and wondered what motive her father might have for sending him. Rosemary had an idea that she knew why, and felt very anxious.

Suddenly they all heard thundering strides on the back verandah, only seconds before the door burst open and Harrison strode in, looking at them all with cold fury.

"What happened to the colt?" he demanded.

Rosemary spoke up quickly, but with perfect composure:

"The wild horses came down, almost to the homestead. They set him off . . ."

Mrs Bailey started to say:

"Not for seventeen years . . ."

But Harrison took no notice of her. He glowered at Rosemary, saying:

"I'm asking Jessica."

He turned, icily calm, towards his daughter. "A bruise on the near foreleg," he said evenly, "black soil from a bottom paddock still in the hooves, *and* a girth mark on the horse. What does that add up to, Jessica?"

Jessica felt words chasing themselves around inside her head. For a second, a ray of sunlight lighting up the plates and the cups hanging on the hooks of the dresser distracted her, seemed to offer calmness and hope. She heard her aunt trying to come to her rescue:

"Your old friend is still alive." Harrison looked puzzled, and Rosemary went on: "The stallion—he was leading the brumbies."

Jessica saw a haunted look come into her father's face, and suddenly she felt that uncomfortable contact with mystery again. Feeling thoroughly on edge by this time, she went on peeling the potatoes.

Harrison recovered himself, the haunted look leaving his face, and his anger began to boil.

"Who rode the colt?" he fired at Jessica, his manner threatening.

"We were breaking him in."

"*We*?" Harrison's anger was white-hot, his face set and stiff.

Jessica straightened herself up, and spoke with a simple pride in the truth.

"Jim's very good with horses."

Harrison stood still for a moment, rage burning in his eyes. Then he thumped the deal table with his fist, and his voice was filled with scorn:

"That mountain boy . . ."

"Now wait, Father," Jessica said desperately. "It wasn't his fault. He was driving the colt when the brumbies came down . . . he went to save the stockhorses . . . " But her courage began to collapse. As soon as she had spoken, she knew how silly her words sounded.

"What stupidity!" Harrison roared. "He saves stockhorses worth a few shillings, and risks a colt worth a thousand pounds!"

Fighting back tears, Jessica said weakly:

"It happened too suddenly."

"Suddenly! Well, suddenly he's finished here!"

Harrison said, thumping the table again. "He gets off this place the moment he gets back." He turned to Rosemary, her face still and pale.

"There's a train tomorrow. Be on it, Rosemary, and take Jessica with you. She will go to a ladies' boarding school."

Tears now running down her cheeks, Jessica cried out:

"No! I won't go!"

Harrison stepped up to her and slapped her hard across the face.

"You are as deceitful as your mother!" he shouted, and the words seemed to whip round and round the kitchen.

Sobbing, Jessica ran from the room, Mrs Bailey following her. But Rosemary stood her ground, as she had always stood her ground against Harrison, never giving in. She spoke now with an icy anger.

"You wouldn't dare break the spirit of that colt the way you've just crushed your own daughter."

"*My* daughter? You really believe that?" Harrison's bitter anger matched her own.

Rosemary stared at him contemptuously.

"Just *when* will you give up this insane obsession?"

"You tell me," he answered. "Matilda was your sister."

Rosemary had herself under control now, and she had one more blow to give.

"You are always so ready to cast blame on other people. Why not look at yourself? What if the night you fired those shots, your aim had been better—what then?"

She had come close to winning the round, but the effort had taken its toll. She knew she would have to compose herself before she went to find Jessica.

Jessica burst out of a side door of the homestead, and ran on, sobbing, across the yard to the stables. Ever since she was a little girl, the stables had been her refuge, and it had been her habit to catch her pony and go for a ride alone, whenever she was in trouble or unhappy. Now, even in the confusion of words and thoughts running around in her head, she was still aware that all the men were busy in the yards, so that no one would be in the stables or barracks.

Kip had been put in his stall. As she took his bridle from its hook, slipped the bit into his mouth, and the headstall over his ears, it was as though she could still hear her father's voice shouting: "You are as deceitful as your mother."

She did up the throatlash with trembling fingers, stopping to wipe away tears. Upset by her sobbing, and her shaking hands, Kip danced away from the saddle, even began to rear.

All the time Jessica kept wondering—what was it that was so wrong at the homestead? What had happened all those years ago? At last the saddle cloth and saddle were settled on Kip's back, and Jessica girthed him up. Leading him out of the stall into the central corridor of the stable, she managed to persuade him to stand still while she swung up into the saddle without getting entangled in the long dress she was still wearing, for she had rushed out without thinking of changing her clothes.

As she rode out into the yard, she said:

"This way, Kip."

All the time she kept asking herself: "Why did the brumbies come? When were they here before?"

Aunt Rosemary had said clearly that the brumby stallion had something to do with her father. In her mind's eye, Jessica saw the huge black stallion rearing above Jim after he had been thrown on to the ground, and saw again the herd galloping out of the trees, manes and tails flying, remembered the thrill of fear which she had felt.

She opened the gate and rode through, reining Kip back to close it. The slab and shingle buildings of the homestead were all distorted by her tears, presenting a strange vision of a place where something mysterious had happened long ago, the consequences of which went on and on—and she felt sure that she was somehow part of it.

As she began to canter, words and pictures came to her, chasing her, as she heard again her father shouting:

"You're as deceitful as your mother", her aunt saying: "Your old friend, the stallion . . ."

How could that great black stallion have such significance in their lives? It had had some power over Jim, too, she knew, for suddenly, on that dreadful morning, he had seemed to be almost in another world, as he galloped the colt and jumped the gate, trying to round up the brumby mob.

Soon hidden in some applebox trees, Jessica let the grey slow to a walk. The stand of applebox curved in a semi-circle away from the house. She rode slowly through them, and pulled up before they went out into the open. There, far ahead, blue and startlingly clear, stood the mountains. Jim was up there, and they might never meet again. Her father was going to sack him, when he brought the cattle back—if, indeed, he ever found what the others had missed.

"It was all my fault," she whispered. "My fault, not Jim's. I should have told Father that it was I who suggested him breaking in the colt."

Without thinking where she was going, she rode off in the direction of the belt of red gums which, stretching right back to the track, hid her from the homestead. She rode on and on. Usually, if she were upset by something, the rhythm of the horse, the scent of the eucalypts and the carolling of the magpies calmed her. This time, the confusion in her mind only seemed to whirl round and round even faster. She was deeply shocked by her father's slap across her face, and disturbed—quite beyond her understanding—by those words which she had barely registered at the time: ". . . as deceitful as your mother." She was also very frightened that her father might really send her away to boarding school. She felt she would far rather run away than let that happen.

She came to the track, all churned up by the cattle returning the day before, and she began thinking of Jim again. She knew that his job was extremely important to him: he had to earn money so that he could go back to his mountain property, but she also felt that there was perhaps something more to the job than just the need for money.

A great flock of currawongs was calling in the trees above her. She barely noticed them, certainly. did not realise that they had arrived down from the mountains only the day before. She sighed. Here she was, feeling desperately that she could not bear to go home, when really she should have been worrying about Jim losing his job.

Slowly the decision formed in her mind to ride on, to warn Jim that he was going to be sacked, to tell him that she was sorry, that it was all her fault. She could not bear to go home now, anyway. Against all reason, she persuaded herself that she would meet Jim on his way back with the cattle.

The currawongs circled above, crying high, wild and free.

Presently the blue and distant hills were on her horizon again, and she and Kip were cantering towards them, scattering cattle, not caring if she upset them, going fast to get away. The track was clearly marked by the hooves of the four hundred cattle. There would be no difficulty in finding the way.

Quite ignorant of the eruption of rage that had boiled over at the now far-away homestead, Jim, leaning forward on Andy's neck, was riding up a steep, rocky slope. He noticed that some of the heath bushes still bore a few of their white-star flowers. He saw the white everlasting daisies moving in the wind.

He had managed to throw off most of his misery about his irresponsible conduct. The sun was warming him, burning through the thin air: there was that clean, sharp scent from the crushed leaves of the mint bushes as his horse trod among them. The mint bushes, the prostanthera, were still flowering, still partly covered with their little, pale-mauve lipped flowers. Jim was smiling for joy at being amongst it all.

They reached the top of the ridge and he sat down in his saddle again, taking a deep, long breath of the wind that blew off the highest peaks. An immense cleft of a river was below him—a river that flowed into the Snowy. He must go along the ridge to the south now, and then he would not have very far to go to find the little warm hollow below the rocks, an hour or so's ride. It was odd that no one had mentioned to him before the little rough holding yard which he had come across, or the bark humpy. Jim had no idea who had built them, but he thought they might come in handy if he did find the cattle. After all, the currawongs had said that snow was coming . . .

As the morning wore on, a strange metallic appearance spread over the sky, and the rising wind began "talking" in the snow gums. Jim was not worried. He was prepared for anything—except snow-shoeing the cattle out. He patted Andy's neck. Presently he noted darkening clouds.

There were rocks above him, and a peaceful looking valley below which opened towards lower country. "That would be a get-away for the cattle if heavy snow really came," he murmured to himself. "I guess this is the place."

He sat perfectly still, peering through the snow gums to the slopes below him. Yes, there was a patch of red hide showing through those thick leaves, and part of a white stripe; there was a horn shining in a ray of light that came from beneath a lowering cloud; there was a white Hereford face staring at him, and another, and another, all of them hard to see at first glance and only just visible.

"Now all we need is Spur's butterfly net," Jim whispered to Andy as, slowly, quietly, he edged the horse round to the south side of them, cutting off their escape, collecting them into a mob before they realised that they were being mustered, then urging them along a cattle pad that followed the direction in which he wanted them to go.

The clouds were gathering around the mountains, as though from nowhere, simply emerging from the metallic sky, almost as though summoned up by the currawong song.

Jessica barely noticed that the sun had vanished. She was riding through a forest of dead trees. They rose straight and tall around her—ribbon gums and candlebarks, burnt and killed by a bush fire which must have raged through these parts some years before, now bleached almost white, like slender, etched ghosts. The great, wide cattle track had split up into many smaller tracks, but she was still on a pad of sorts perhaps even a wombats' highway, though cattle had also walked there.

The fire that had killed those trees must have started low down and roared its way upwards from the valley floor, right up into the mountain ash: Jessica and Kip, climbing, climbing, soon found themselves in the vaulted aisles of the grey, dead ash, with no bark streamers to blow and sigh in the strong wind, just the creak of dead limbs and the pencilled outlines of the trees towering against black clouds.

Jessica did not even notice that it had become cold, though her dress and light woollen coat were small protection.

Jim, much higher up in the mountains, weaving his little mob of cattle along a narrow pad among the snow gums, did begin to feel the cold. The wind was sweeping through the twisted branches, and the cattle kept trying to turn away from it.

He started to push them along a little faster, hoping to get them into that yard of snow gum branches and forked logs he had discovered before the weather became too rough. He hunched his shoulders against the cold, feeling his bruised muscles stiffening.

Soon he undid the straps that held his oilskin coat to the pummel of his saddle, dismounted for a brief moment and put it on. The wind billowed it around him unmanageably. As he mounted Andy again, he saw the first flake of snow drift down and land on his sleeve, a small white star against the brown material.

The trees began to lash around. Another flake fell, cold on his face, and he felt a surging thrill of joy in the snow, in the white flakes that were now like a blowing curtain in the sky. But it was time to hurry his cattle even more. He uncoiled his whip, and held it loosely. He knew that the calmer he could keep them, the better.

Chapter Nine

On the Cliff in the Wind and the Snow

The climb through the mountain ash was very steep and rough, and Kip was tiring. Jessica pulled him up on a flatter part of the spur, just where the snow gums started, to let him get his breath.

They both jumped as two black cockatoos came hurtling past on the wind, screaming as they banked through the wind-swirled trees. Kip stood with legs splayed, shaking with fear, and Jessica's heart was pounding. The two birds vanished in the trees, but their screams sounded on and on through the forest, and the clouds, and the wind. It did not seem to be the time to stop. Clouds were flying around them. Kip had become very nervous.

Jessica suddenly knew she was cold, but the track led on, actually marked slightly more clearly. She could not go back. She put her hand up to her face where her father had slapped her. She would not go back; she would not go to boarding school; she *must* find Jim and tell him what had happened, tell him she was sorry.

For the last hour, Kip's footfalls had been saying: "Must find Jim, must find Jim."

Pulling her jacket around her, Jessica urged Kip onwards. A snowflake touched her face and melted, and she shivered with fright. Then Kip slipped on a wet rock, gave an odd-sounding snort of fear, and stopped dead. A frightened uncertainty began to rise within Jessica, invade her from all around. She looked up at the sky: it was grey, almost tinged with pink, and a few flakes, like white feathers, were drifting, circling, falling through the air way on high.

"There's a stockman's hut on this track," she whispered to Kip. "I won't go back. I must find Jim." She pushed him on and on, up another long, steep ridge, as she leant forward in the saddle. The clouds came in thicker, blown on the wind, and the snowflakes fell faster, beginning to collect and lie on the ground.

At the top of the ridge Jessica dismounted to give Kip another spell; she peered through the clouds and the driving flakes. Occasionally the clouds blew apart and, through the fast-falling snow, she saw mountains and more mountains, crags, rocks piled upon rocks, and voids so filled with fog that she could not tell how deep they were.

She leant against Kip. He was steaming, and the flakes melted as they touched him, but the snow felt cold on her hands and face. Reality beat at her with the wind-driven flakes. The horror of the scene in the homestead slid into the background. She was in the mountains, caught in a snowstorm: alone, and in great danger.

Jessica mounted again—so wet and cold that she did not feel the snow on her saddle soaking through her clothes. Now the fog and the clouds and the falling snow closed in absolutely. Kip kept fighting to turn his rump into the storm. Nothing could be seen except the whipping branches of the occasional snow gums that grew on that exposed plateau.

The wind howled and tore at her. Her hair was soaked, and hanging in long wet streamers around her. She tried to force Kip on, but they were going round in circles. She dismounted and started to walk, pulling him after her.

Then a great blast of wind-driven snow hit them, full on, and thunder rolled and crashed. Kip pulled back sharply, slipped and fell, then sprang up, pulling Jessica over. She hung on to the reins, but then a branch whipped Kip and he reared, dragging the reins out of her hand. She leapt up, tripping over her skirt, and grabbed the reins again, calling him.

Terrified, the grey plunged towards her, knocking her backwards. As she was struggling up he pulled back again, wresting the reins from her hands, and then vanished into the snowstorm. Earth gave way under Jessica's boots and, just as she heard the drum beat of Kip's galloping hooves getting fainter in the distance, she went slithering and sliding down the face of a smooth, wet rock. Her fingers strived for a hold, but she kept on slipping, down, down into the boiling, black clouds.

Her slide stopped suddenly as she landed on flat rock. The clouds were dense around her. Bracing herself against the rock face, she slowly got to her feet, feeling outwards with one hand. There was nothing, just empty space. Something about the feel of the air warned her not to step forward. She pressed back against the rock down which she had slipped, then turned to face it.

She realised that she would have to try to climb upwards, but, peering through the fog and exploring for hand-holds with her fingers, she found that the rock face in front of her was almost entirely smooth and polished by wind and weather, giving no grip. The wind howled and boomed with a hollow sound in the void behind her.

She turned round again, pressing her back against the rock. Then big flakes began to fall—thick, beating flakes that poured through the grey clouds, moving, always moving. She began to feel giddy and terribly afraid. A pair of gang-gangs went flying through the shroud of falling snow—grey spectres. Snow began to cover her . . . She spread her arms out along the wall, fingers hard against the rock. This was not fear, but terror.

Later, before night closed in, the clouds blew apart briefly, though the snow still fell. Jessica had sunk down against the rock face at last, and, as the clouds broke, she sprang up to see if there was a way to climb down or around. She looked, and she screamed.

Below her was a drop of thousands of feet. She was on a rock shelf with a huge drop below her, and no one in the world knew where she was. Slowly the dark of the night flowed into the depth below.

There were tough, gnarled branches of the immensely enduring alpine plum pine growing out of a big crack at one end of the rock shelf. As darkness crept upwards, Jessica wedged herself between those branches and the rock face. The branches seemed strong. She felt sure they would hold her to the rock, even if she grew dizzy, even if, by any chance, she went to sleep and had a nightmare. But, she thought, she was much too cold—and far too frightened—to sleep, and her mind seemed almost out of control, wildly circling round all that had happened.

The night closed in. Sometimes rain fell, sometimes snow. As Jessica sat huddled on the rock, she thought more and more of the days of breaking in the colt. She was very cold, and shivering uncontrollably. Gradually even the shivering stopped: she knew that no one might ever find her, she knew she might die. A strange thought came to her—if she died, the mystery back at the homestead might cease to be—or might cease to matter. It might simply be easier to die . . .

But the warmth of those days in the yards—just she and Jim, and the colt—kept coming back to her. She knew quite clearly why she had come to the mountains.

Jim was several miles away. In spite of the falling snow, he had a good fire going and his quart pot was boiling. He threw in some tea leaves, let the quart pot bubble for a second, then took it from the fire. Setting it on the ground, he tapped it with his boot to make the leaves settle. He looked round with a feeling of satisfaction. The bark humpy, close by, was fairly rain-proof, and the cattle were all penned in and huddled together, making no effort to break out. So far he had proved himself capable of doing a good job.

Old Spur thought he should stick it out, down there. Perhaps he was right. It had certainly been wonderful working with Jessica, breaking in the colt. It would not be likely that he would often get a chance to work with Jess, but still, she would be about. Maybe it would not be too bad after all, staying on. Maybe the old man would give up trying to put him down all the time. As for Curly, he'd fix Curly himself.

Jim did wonder about the colt, once or twice, and whether Harrison had found out that he had already been broken in, and, if so, how the old man had taken it. He wondered, too, if Harrison had discovered that Jim had galloped the colt after the brumbies. Jessica had been so angry with him. Some day he might get a chance to explain to her about that brumby stallion and the death of his father.

From time to time it rained, sometimes snow fell softly, and always the wind howled around the peaks higher up. But Jim and his cattle were comfortably sheltered.

Back at Harrison's station, the rain had not come as quickly as it had in the mountains, and so they had got their branding done.

The men did not know that Jessica had not come in for lunch. Both Rosemary and Mrs Bailey were anxious, but they were used to her going out on her own and neither dreamt that she had gone far. They were only worrying about a hurt and miserable girl who did not want to come back to the homestead.

By mid-afternoon the heavy clouds had gathered, making it very dark. When Harrison came in, asked for Jessica and received the cold reply that she had gone out and had not come back, he took no notice for a while, expecting her to return to the house as darkness fell. If anything, he was angry rather than worried. Angry with himself, and angry with Jessica for being so childish as to go out for this long.

Suddenly it was dark, and suddenly he was frantic. He sent for Kane and ordered him to get the men ready to make up a search party. Kane was a little put out by this instruction:

"The men've been drinking," he said. "They started, a bit, when we got back with the cattle, and now that the calf branding's done, they've been properly stuck into it for several hours."

"The weather's turning bad," Harrison said. "They've got to help find her quickly."

"They're not going to be any use," Kane pointed out.

"What!" roared Harrison.

"The men are drunk," Kane repeated. "They're not going to be any use to us."

Harrison fixed Kane with a fierce look that made him falter.

"They must be ready to ride in ten minutes," Harrison said. Kane knew he meant it.

"Yes sir!"

The barracks were pitch dark when Kane walked in. The only sounds were snores and mutterings made by men in their sleep. Kane held his lantern up and banged on the wall with a broom handle.

"Everybody up!" he yelled.

There was no response. He held the lantern to the face on the first bunk. A tall stockman was right out to it. Then Kane turned to Moss and shook him as hard as he could. As Moss groaned, Kane shook him harder.

"Moss, quick! You've got five minutes to get dressed and be outside." Then Kane grabbed Curly, pulling him right out of his bunk. Curly, still dressed, but full of grog, made a wild swing at him. Kane tripped him up, and Curly slammed head-first into the timber wall, sinking to the floor, out cold.

"God help us," Kane muttered, and headed for Frew, shaking the older man more gently.

"Come on old man," he said. "I need you."

Frew sat straight up and made a grab for his rifle:

"I tell you I'm not goin'. He shot first. You're not takin' me in."

Kane picked up a billy of water and doused him. Frew slowly came to.

"You want to be careful what you say in your sleep, Frew," Kane warned him. "Anyhow, get up now. Jessica's gone and got herself lost. I need a tracker and you're it."

"I can't even see enough to find me boots."

"Well, go without them. You've got five minutes."

Kane did not dare leave the barracks. He knew the men would never get moving if he did not stay to chivvy them along. The tall stockman was cursing; a short stockman was grumbling; Moss was reeling round, almost useless but somehow getting his kit together. Frew was at last lacing on his boots, buckling up leggings. Curly lay quite still.

Kane hurried them on.

"Get moving," he ordered. "She's got to be found before this storm gets worse."

"It'll be snowing in the mountains," Frew muttered.

The overseer almost drove them out of the barracks. By now Curly had come to and pulled on boots, hat, and oilskin. In the stables, Harrison sat on his grey thoroughbred, stern, immobile as a statue.

"Thou shalt not bow down to them," said the short stockman loudly, as though still reading his beloved Bible.

"The horses are in the yard. Catch them and saddle up," Kane ordered. Amid much ill-humoured muttering and in the spattering rain, horses were caught and saddled by fumbling fingers. Here and there an aching head leant against a horse's warm shoulder as the girth was done up.

They all mounted and followed the man with the face carved in lines of anger, anxiety and unhappiness, out along the track in the beating rain.

The rain had been falling for some time, but Kip's hoof marks were still visible, going into the stand of applebox. Frew had got himself under control quicker than the other men, all of whom were swaying in their saddles and mumbling imprecations, but when a barn owl suddenly flew, screaming, out of a hollow in an applebox, the old stockman let out a startled cry.

This cheered the others a little, but it was still Frew who, on foot, leading his horse and holding a lantern, tracked Kip onwards through the applebox trees and the red gums, towards the track. And there, heading straight for the mountains, were Kip's hoof marks.

Frew got on his horse, and they rode along the path marked out by the four hundred cattle. Occasionally Harrison or Frew dismounted, lit a lantern again, and checked to make sure that Kip's hoof marks still headed in the same direction.

The rain became heavier and heavier, but, as low as this, no snow fell.

Harrison felt extremely anxious now. Perhaps he had driven Jessica to this . . . Rosemary had pointed that out to him very forcibly. Worried and angry, he rode on. The night was very cold, and would be far colder higher up. *Where was she?*

Sometimes they called, sending cooees ringing through the pitch black night. Going on was really useless, for no track could be picked up at all now, yet they went on. At dawn, Frew could still find no hoof marks on the rain-washed ground, and another huge storm was brewing, though the morning broke fine.

Jim woke before dawn. He stirred the fire, which he had kept going all night, and boiled his quart pot. At first light he saddled his horse and let the cattle out of the makeshift yard, driving them along a faint pad. He whistled a tune to himself as he watched his little mob and kept an eye on the weather. The sun soon melted what snow still lay on the ground, except where it had fallen in the shade of logs and rocks.

All of a sudden something on the track seemed odd. For a few strides he did not check his horse, but kept looking back at the ground over which they had just walked. Then he stopped and rode back, dismounted and studied the ground. Brushing aside some twigs, he found himself looking at the hoof prints of a shod horse.

He began to follow the prints. They went right off the track, and, even though they were often almost washed away by the rain, he knew they were made by a terrified, galloping horse.

Sometimes bushes hid the hoof marks, but the bushes themselves were torn and broken, showing where the horse had burst through them.

"It galloped in front of last night's storm," Jim thought. Then he saw the shod hoof marks again, very clearly, and knew it was not a very big horse. From one lot of marks, he guessed that it had nearly fallen, that it was out of control with terror, and was also very tired. Slowly it filtered into Jim's mind, from all he had observed, that this horse had not often been away from smooth country, and that it possibly had no rider. An uneasy feeling began to flow through him—nothing quite explicable.

He stopped. The tracks had ended abruptly, right at the edge of a small, rocky cliff. Jim rode a few strides forward and looked over the edge. The drop was about ten feet, and there were rocks covered over with bushes down below. Hoping his cattle would not stray too far, he rode round to the base of the cliff.

For a moment or so he could see nothing—no tracks, no place where a horse had landed. Then he felt a strange sensation, like a cold, hard hand clutching at his heart and lungs. There was a patch of grey hide behind a thick clump of heath. Jim forced Andy through the bushes.

Kip was lying in a twisted heap—quite dead.

"Kip!" he gasped, and the fear that had been lurking not far below his consciousness rushed upwards as the full implication of finding the dead horse flashed into his mind.

"Jessica! Jessica!" he called.

He began searching through the bushes, combed them, called again. There was no sign of her anywhere near. He swung back on to Andy, started back-tracking Kip, cantering, leaning out of the saddle, the better to see the rain-washed hoof marks. He kept on calling, apprehensive, wondering if Jessica were alive, or dead, or unconscious. Then he slowed down, in case he missed her, or did not hear her call.

The tracks were not easy to follow, but he reckoned Kip had got away from her, and that he should find the place where it had happened.

Jessica was stiff and cold, and aching all over, but she had survived the night, huddled between the cliff and the tough little branches. As the dawn came, and the fog and clouds rolled away, she steeled herself to look over the edge again, to see if there were any possible way of escape. But there was absolutely no way down off that shelf.

In desperation she tried once more to feel for hand-holds on the smooth cliff face. There were a few little crevices, from one of which hung a small plant of stackhousia, still with two or three of its strongly scented golden stars left from summer. With fingers pressed into the cracks, she pulled herself up a few feet and found another hand-hold a little higher. The toes of her boots were clinging on to a small rough patch on the rock.

She reached out for another rough patch for her fingers to grip. But there was nothing, just smooth, polished rock. She tried again, pressing herself up against the surface. Still nothing. There *had* to be something, she thought frantically, she couldn't go back down. She pushed off with her feet, praying that a little higher up she would find a grip. There was no grip at all.

She was sliding backwards, losing her contact with the rock face. She screamed. Then her feet were on the shelf again. As she landed, she almost over-balanced, swaying towards the edge and feeling the pull of that terrible drop. She forced herself back against the cliff and made a wild grab at one of her hand-holds. Then she sank down against the rock face, sobbing.

Her heart thundered, pounded; her whole body was

shaking. Her face was pressed into the gravelly rock of the shelf. She might never see Jim again, never see anyone. Gradually the pounding of fear through her body quietened, and the first rays of the sun, touching the cliff, began to warm her.

For a while she slept, a queer, uneasy sleep, for she was conscious all the time of the yawning space below her, as she clutched tight one of the tenacious branches of the alpine plum pine.

The ominous cawing of crows woke her, and then she heard another sound. Hope flared up. It was the ring of a horse's shoe striking rock.

She screamed: "Help! Help!" over and over again.

All she could hear was her cry echoing round and round the rocks. She stopped calling, and listened. As the echoes died away, becoming fainter and fainter, she heard the sound of pebbles sliding and bouncing down the rock above her, and she was suddenly showered by gravel.

Then the handle of a stockwhip came swinging down towards her.

Chapter Ten

An Enchanted Snow Gum Grove

Jim led Jessica away from the cliff top, and from the sight of that huge depth below. He barely even registered that he had held her in his arms when he pulled her over the top of the rock. All he knew was that he must get her away from that exposed place and in amongst the snow gums where he could light a fire quickly, and find water with which to make her a hot drink. He was well aware of the danger she had been in—not only the danger of falling, but also the danger from the cold, and the wind on her body after the snow and the rain. The risk was still there if he did not soon get a hot drink into her, get her warm and dry.

There was a little grove of snow gums not far away, and a pool of last night's rain held in a rock basin. Jim hitched up his horse and pulled the blanket that he had been using as a saddle cloth out from under his saddle.

"Take off your wet clothes quickly," he said, "and wrap up in this. I'll get a fire going."

It was only a matter of moments before he had a fire burning, and, while Jessica undressed, he built it up into quite a blaze. Jessica, from behind a bushy snow gum, talked and talked without ceasing, as she struggled with her saturated boots, and peeled off her wet clothes. Jim listened to her anxiously, while carefully tending the quart pot and unwrapping a little of Spur's homemade bread and some cold beef for her to eat. She sounded so wound up, as though a spring must surely break.

He was relieved when he heard her voice getting calmer—but bothered by the story she told. He knew it was his fault that she had got into so much trouble. She was saying that she was sorry, that it was her fault for encouraging him to break in the colt.

"So that's it," he said over his shoulder to the invisible girl undressing behind the snow gum, after he had heard the full story of her father's fury. "No more working for the old . . . for your father. Never thought I'd be sorry about that, but I am."

His voice trailed off into silence as Jessica emerged, clutching the blanket round her, her wet hair hanging in ropes around her face and over her shoulders. She was carrying her clothes and boots in a fairly awkward bundle so that the blanket seemed at great risk of slipping off her.

Jim, feeling hopelessly shy, took the wet clothes and boots and draped them on logs near the fire. Then he made her sit on a bleached snow gum trunk, close to the blaze, to get warm.

"Why are you sorry?" she asked.

"I'll miss seeing you," he said simply, without looking at her, thinking back on all the shared days of breaking in the colt, the closeness between them as they worked, the flash as though there had been sparks when their arms touched. But his anxiety for Jessica, after such a night of bitter cold, became urgent once more, and a nagging worry crept over him too—the possibility of losing those cattle, spoiling the good job he had done.

Jessica was torn between her terrible memories of the night on the cliff, which still shook her, and her immense relief at being rescued. After she had walked out from the snow gums, and sat down on the log, her hysterical talking had subsided. Now she said in a low voice:

"It all seemed so clear, when I was trapped on that

cliff: now I don't know how to say it clearly . . . Jim, I was so frightened . . . I did such a lot of thinking . . . I don't want to go back." Her voice rose uncontrollably: "Jim, I'm not going back."

Jim was so startled that he momentarily forgot his anxieties.

"Come on, Jess," he said, sitting down on the log beside her. "You'll feel better about everything when you've had a good hot drink and rested a bit."

Jessica was trembling, not only from cold and exhaustion, but also from the whirlwind of emotions that so often follows an experience of being in tremendous danger. She put a hand on Jim's sleeve.

"I was so frightened," she repeated. "Then —later—it didn't seem to matter much if I died . . . Everything was such a mess. But, still I wanted to see you again—be with you. Somehow I began to feel sure you'd come—so I hung on until you came . . . All I wanted was to be with you."

Jim was gazing at her, his young face serious, blue eyes wide, but he could not find any words to say. He realised sharply that he had been in love with her almost since that afternoon tea at the homestead, but that he had pushed away his longing for her because she was Harrison's daughter, and because whatever future he had, for himself, was a long way off. He turned away from her at last, threw some tea leaves into the quart pot, then lifted it carefully from the fire.

"I've got to take you back, Jess," he said as he tapped his quart pot with a stick.

The words, together with his matter-of-fact action, seemed to snap her control. Her answer was almost screamed:

"I'm not going back."

Jim poured some tea into the lid of the quart, opening out its handles to make it into a mug. Experienced in the effects of wind on a body soaked by snow and rain, he knew how vital it was for her to take some hot tea and food.

"Please sip this." Handing it to her, he added: "They'll be worried sick about you."

"I don't care if they are."

Jim sat down beside her again, on the age-old, bleached log. He took a deep breath and then spoke very quietly:

"There'll be men out looking for you, risking their lives. Anyhow," he added, "I've got to take the cattle down. I can't stay away."

He knew, immediately, that he should not have said that.

"Haven't you been listening to me?" she shouted, her lips trembling. Then her last particle of control went, and she began to cry.

"We would only get into more trouble, if we stayed away," Jim said quietly. But Jessica hardly heard him—she was still, perhaps, in her own mind, on the ledge of the cliff.

"Please have a sip of tea, Jess," he begged. He sat, feeling helpless. He had not known many girls of his own age, and never, since childhood days, had he seen one cry—and he loved this one desperately.

"Come on, Jess darling, please drink some tea."

He saw her hands shaking as she lifted the quart pot lid, and he watched her sip, trying not to burn her trembling lips on the tin. Perhaps it would steady her if she realised that he would not act irresponsibly, would not let her father down again.

"It's just that I have to finish this job," he said. "I'll take you to Spur's place, and then come back for the cattle."

He broke off a little piece of the bread and gave it to her, then ate a little himself, to encourage her.

The tea, the shared bread, and the heat from the red coals of their fire were beginning to warm Jessica. She was still shaking with deep sobs, but Jim's words—"I'll have to finish this job"—finally sank into her consciousness. As she sat, trying to sip tea between convulsive shudders, the memory of them both sitting on the rails of the colt's yards slid into her mind, and she remembered Jim saying how he had to earn the right to return to his own place.

"I'm sorry," she said, between sobs. "Everything seemed so clear, when I was on the cliff." She fixed miserable eyes on Jim. "But it never is, is it?"

Awkwardly Jim patted her blanket-covered knee, searching for the right words. Then Jessica leant back against him, looking up, the tears making white runnels down the dirt on her face.

Jim felt her body against his, felt its warmth and softness. Battling for control, he put an uncertain hand on her shoulder. He knew that nearly all she had said was illogical, hysterical, but one thing shone out as truth—that she loved him.

"I'm sorry, too," he said. Then suddenly she was in his arms, and he was burying his face in her hair, kissing her. It had been as though Jessica had been cut off from him, in a world of her own, but now, in his arms, she was entirely real.

A wind stirred the topmost leaves of the snow gums, and the clouds had cleared away from the mountain peaks. Jim opened his eyes and there, above Jessica's head, stood the enduring reality of the mountains, of the snow-powdered granite crags.

Jessica lay back against him for a moment, her head tucked beneath his chin, looking at their enchanted circle of snow gums, at the golden everlastings that grew in the grass, and the few remaining gentianella. The frail song of a robin redbreast sounded from a tree.

"We are alone, except for the robin," she whispered, turning to kiss him again. The smoke from their snow gum fire wove faintly around them on an eddy of wind, binding them together in enchantment.

Jessica's clothes had dried and she dressed again. Jim refolded the blanket that had covered her beautiful body, saddled up his horse, doused the fire and strapped on the quart pot again.

"You ready now?" he asked, almost shyly. He had

not yet told her about Kip, and hoped she might just think that he had made his way home. His own horse was going to have to carry them both.

When they were both mounted, Jim leant forward and stroked Andy's ears.

"Go well," he urged. "You've got Jess on your back, too."

And so the little horse bore his double burden, up and down steep slopes, through boggy patches, over rough rocks. He carried them through snow gum forests, and steeply through the high-towering ash, where gang-gangs flew between the huge trunks. Jim and Jessica, their bodies and spirits fired with an intense longing, rode below those great trees whose sun-glittering crowns reached up to the brilliant sky.

No longer was Jessica bowed down with misery, as she had been when she rode up into the mountains. Now she saw, she heard, and she felt everything with a profound clarity, each image or sound fitting into the mosaic of her happiness, making it greater, and her happiness making each sight and sound more beautiful. The great mountain ash that formed a vault across the aisles along which they rode and filled the air with the magnificent eucalypt scent of their leaves, bruised by last night's storm; the silver snow gums, tall and slender on the fringe of the ash forest but soon becoming a maze of twisted branches on the higher, unprotected slopes—both became part of this mosaic.

A white-throated warbler's marvellous cadence rose clear and sweet through the trees. Jim pulled Andy up to a stop:

"Listen," he whispered. "It must be on its way north for the winter. It's singing for you, Jess."

Holding tightly to him, Jessica pressed her face into his back, feeling his closeness even more strongly.

In the snowgrass among those wind-tormented trees, there were still some late-flowering pale vanilla lilies, and here and there, some eye-brights—white and lilac, even a few of a deep blue-purple.

Jim pointed to a patch, saying:

"See, Jess, they are nearly the colour of your eyes." He turned and smiled, putting his hand gently on to her knee.

The snow gums became smaller, more pressed down to the grass and the rocks, as they reached the top of the spur, and then there was nothing between them and the sunlit sweep of the high mountains. Glittering patches of snow lay in pockets or in long streaks. The great rock tors were still powdered silver-white, clear-cut against the sky. Jim pulled up for Jessica to see it all, clear of cloud. She sat quietly for a time, silenced by the splendour, and then said simply:

"Jim, it's beautiful."

"Yes," Jim said, his eyes, his whole face alight with joy. "But," and he pointed to rolling black clouds that were approaching from the north-west, "wait till that gets here. We'd better hurry on to Spur's house."

Jessica saw the cloud and was far more awake to its presence—and its meaning—than she had been the day before:

"It changes so suddenly, doesn't it? One minute it's paradise, the next it's trying to kill you," she shivered, snuggling into Jim's back.

"Yep, that's the way it is, up here. But if it was easy to get to know, there'd be—there'd be no challenge—no reward . . ." He was seeking the right words. "You've got to treat the mountains like a high-spirited horse—never take them for granted." He turned his head to look at Jessica.

She nodded, looking deeply into his eyes, eyes that seemed to her to hold the mountains, the sky, and the snow.

"It's the same with people," she murmured, and leant forward to kiss him.

They were alone up there against the sky, encircled by the mountains Jim loved so dearly. He pressed his mouth to Jessica's. The first wind of the approaching storm ruffled his fair hair, touched their faces and bodies, binding them even closer together.

Andy, feeling the touch of the wind, pricked his ears and moved a little.

Jim whispered:

"We must go, Jess."

He turned back into the saddle, patted Andy's neck, and pressed him into an amble along the winding cattle pad on the ridge top, hoping to race the storm.

Spur, having stopped outside his hut to enjoy the scent of the early morning after the storm, and only giving a cursory thought as to where Jim might be, had then gone to his mine and spent most of the day at the end of the shaft which he had driven into the hill, fossicking and, as ever, mumbling to himself. Now he had a few quartz samples in his hand and was examining them by the light of his lantern. Suddenly he threw them down in a fury.

"Gone! Nothing! No colour!" Raising his arms aloft, he bellowed into the gloom.

"Jezebel!" Picking up his hammer, he aimed a hefty swipe at the props.

There was a bang, as loud and sudden as the sound of a gun shot, and a cross beam above his head crashed to the ground, narrowly missing him. Looking up in horror as rocks started to fall, Spur turned to run, with the best turn of speed that his peg-leg could manage, down the tunnel. But it seemed that the rock falls were chasing him, and certainly gaining.

"I didn't mean it," he yelled, just as he tripped on a stone and fell full length into a puddle on the floor. Putting his arms over his head, he shut his eyes tightly, waiting to be buried, as the rocks started tumbling down on to his body.

Rumble and crash! Thud, thud! As the rocks fell, Spur muttered prayers and imprecations. Then there was a silence. Cautiously, Spur opened an eye and rolled on to his back. The lantern was still alight beside him. He just lay there, rather bruised and shocked, still scared to move. Then his eyes opened wider and wider, with that strange, wild look of his.

There, in the roof above, was a small vein of shining gold in a bed of quartz.

"Why, you old—" he began, and then his tone changed to one of tenderness. "You lovely creature!" he whispered. "That's what you've been trying to tell me, all these years. It was up there, all the time." He pushed himself up on to his good leg, and walked, a little stiffly, but straight-backed, to the tunnel entrance. It was barely twenty feet away—after twenty years of driving that shaft further and further into the mountain.

It was time to get to work.

The wind was whipping the branches around, tossing leaves and twigs about, as Jessica and Jim rode up to Spur's hut. Though it was only late afternoon, once again heavy cloud was bringing darkness very quickly. It felt like winter already. Just momentarily, as the wind dropped, there came the sweet scent of the first flowers on the black sallee trees.

Jim was puzzled. No smoke rose from the crooked chimney, and the hut seemed to be enfolded in an unusual silence. He yelled:

"Spur, Spur!" But there was no answer. Jim cursed.

Jessica, staring wide-eyed at the crazy, haphazard building, asked:

"Who is this Spur?"

Jim looked at her in surprise. "Spur? I thought you knew him."

"No. Why should I?"

Quickly, Jim decided that his answer had better wait, at least until he had found the old man.

"You slide off, and wait here, Jess," he said. "Get inside out of the wind, and I'll go down to the creek to see if I can find him." Even Jim did not know the exact whereabouts of the well-hidden mine.

He held Jessica steady while she slithered down. As she patted Andy for a moment and rubbed her face on his shoulder, Jim bent and kissed the top of her head.

Left alone outside the strange house, with the icy cold wind hurtling around her, Jessica stepped hesitantly up on to the porch, pushed the door open and peered inside. Then she walked in, tentatively, but glad to be out of the wind. Suddenly she felt very tired.

Moving around inside, peering into the gloom of the hut, she was amused at all Spur's labour-saving gadgets. She lifted the lid of the stew pot, sniffed, and took a step back. Just as Jim appeared in the doorway, announcing that Spur was not at the creek, her eye lighted on the velvet frame on the windowsill. She picked it up, and stared at it—and her eyes widened in disbelief.

The velvet frame surrounded a dageurreotype of a face that seemed to be her own—and yet, it was not her own. She was utterly bewildered. The face in the old photograph was hers, but perhaps a little older; the clothes were decidedly old-fashioned.

As Jim lit a lamp, a reflection of her face appeared in the dusty windowpane against the dark of the wild evening outside. It was extraordinary—her face and the face within the velvet frame were nearly identical. Jessica was suddenly overwhelmed by a strange sensation of being lost entirely, almost as though she had ceased to exist. Then she turned to Jim, seeking her very identity in his arms.

"What is it?" he asked, enfolding her against his body.

The beat of galloping hooves sounded outside, followed by a series of yells and cooees and cheers. Jim knew immediately it was Spur.

Then the old man's voice rang out as he saw Jim's horse tied to the fence:

"Jim! Jim Craig! Hey Jim, my boy!" and another wild cooee echoed round the hills and was caught by the wind and carried away.

Spur clumped his way into the hut, holding a heavy-looking gunny sack in his hand. His face, his eyes, his hat, his hair, his clothing—everything—looked wilder than usual. He was laughing.

"They said Spur was mad," he said, between great

bursts of laughter.

"Are you all right?" Jim asked, laughing too.

"I've never been better . . ." But Spur's answer broke off as he became aware of Jessica, standing perfectly still, framed by the small window, her face softly lit by one of those oblique shafts of light from beneath the storm clouds. Spur was silenced. It seemed to him as if his velvet-framed picture was there . . . larger . . . come to life . . .

His voice came in a whisper:

"Matilda . . . I found the gold." But the statement sounded almost like a question.

Jessica, thoroughly puzzled, spoke to him:

"I'm Jessica . . . Jessica Harrison."

There was silence again, as Spur slowly came back from a time twenty years past into the wind-tossed present.

"Ah—ah Jessica. You look like your—you look real grown up," he sighed at last.

Jessica did not move. As the look of crazy excitement left Spur's face, his strong likeness to her father suddenly became apparent to her.

She put out her hand to Jim, unconsciously seeking his help in this situation that was beyond her understanding, but which she now realised must be part of the mystery, the sadness that had always lingered in the homestead.

Jim squeezed her hand, trying to help her.

"Jess, this is Spur. I don't know why you don't know it, but . . . he is your uncle, your father's brother."

Stunned, Jessica could not move or say a single word. Spur, however, had recovered his irrepressible buoyancy. He spoke softly, smiling:

"Just one of life's injustices, I guess—you never have a chance to choose your own relations!"

Jessica began to see that perhaps there could be a funny side to this mysterious tangle. A faint smile started to curve the corners of her mouth.

"Uncle?" she asked disbelievingly, still uncertain.

Spur had a mocking look on his face:

"Let this be a lesson to you, Jim. I find a little bit of

gold, and immediately, after all these years, the relations turn up!" And he chuckled.

Then Jessica realised that she still held the velvet-framed dageurreotype in her hand.

"But you have a picture of my mother here," she said questioningly.

Spur thought deeply for a while. The clowning expression faded from his face and, when he spoke, it was no answer at all.

"Well," he said. "The prettiest visitor I've ever had, and not even a cup of tea."

Jessica pleaded:

"Please, what are you trying to hide from me? I'm not a child."

The mystery that had stalked the homestead for as long as she could remember seemed suddenly to flow into the hut, and the wind cried through the black sallee trees with all the aching sorrow of a love that had to end. Jim, sensing her turmoil, put his arm around her, so that the future came in on the wind too, and the memory of a snow gum grove and golden everlastings.

Spur did not reply, but started to fuss around making tea. At last he spoke, and the quiet dignity of his words seemed at odds with his weird clothing and rough hut:

"Jessica," he said, "there's pain and suffering when you try to dig up the past. I'm sorry, but . . ." And both Jessica and Jim knew that they must not push the old man any further.

Jim also knew he must get going. It might take him time to find his cattle and round them up again.

"Spur," he said, "Jess has lost her way and has got to get home, but I've got to go back for the cattle. Can you take her down?"

Spur opened his mouth to say no. Then, as he took in the two of them standing together, holding hands, he pursed his lips together in a soundless whistle.

"Sure, I will," and he nearly added under his breath: "God help you."

"You'll look after her for me, then?" Jim said.

"Oh, I'll look after her," the old man responded, turning affectionately to Jessica, "as if you were my own daughter." He said no more, but the words seemed to fly around the hut, moth-winged, yet indestructible.

Jim walked to the door.

"If the cattle have not roamed too far, I shouldn't be far behind you," he smiled at Jessica. "And don't touch his wallaby stew."

"You ungrateful tyke," Spur roared, as Jim went out of the hut. "Anyway, there won't be wallaby tonight. I'll kill the fatted calf." He stopped and thought for a moment. "Come to think of it, I already have," and he laughed at Jessica's querying expression.

The last remnants of daylight were left, but the rain had begun to fall. Jim rode first to a junction of two well-defined tracks and hung a bright handkerchief on a tree, and with it a small canvas bag in which he put a note. Then he went on to find his cattle, hoping that they had kept going downhill, and had not headed back to their valley.

Spur's hut, for all its odd angles, was warm and comfortable. Jessica and Spur set about preparing dinner, chatting all the time.

As Jessica put some vegetables on to cook, she eased her anxiety by telling the old man all about the breaking in of the colt. She was thankful to hear his reassurance that Jim could break in a horse better than anyone he had ever seen. Then she told of the row at the homestead, and her subsequent departure for the mountains . . .

"It was silly, I suppose, but I was so angry and miserable. Then the only thing I could think of was seeing Jim."

Spur was leaping around the hut in his usual jack-in-a-box style.

"No harm done," he said. "What's the sense of being young if you can't be impulsive now and then?"

Jessica was looking around for something.

"Tablecloth?" she asked.

Spur handed her an old newspaper.

"No expense spared, madam, and you can read the news while you're eating."

He started rummaging in a dark cupboard, at last backing out with a very dusty bottle of wine in his hand. He blew off the dust, causing Jessica to sneeze.

"This is *not* to be sneezed at," he said. "They'd charge an extra three guineas for the cobwebs, down in the city."

"Where do I find some glasses?" Jessica looked around again.

"On the shelf." Spur had a perfect poker face.

Behind her, on a shelf, were two solid glasses made from the bottoms of beer bottles after their tops had been cut off by a red-hot wire.

"Why, these must be quite valuable," she said, trying not to laugh.

"Indeed they are—a matched pair," Spur said gravely. He had a very old, very lethal-looking knife in his hand, and he gave her a plate. "Take this plate," he said with impressive dignity, "and follow me to the cool room."

The cool room was a draughty, freezing alcove off the main hut. Spur turned back a screen of hessian. A haunch of beef was hanging up, and with the huge knife, he sliced off two big steaks.

"Do you raise beef?" The laughter was still in Jessica's voice.

"Oh yes," Spur answered. "I'm well known for it. A small and modest herd . . ."

As he turned to put the steaks on the plate which Jessica held out, the lamplight showed up a hide hanging on a rail. It was clearly marked with the letter H within a diamond—Harrison's brand. This time Jessica could not help laughing.

Spur saw what she was looking at, but was not at all disturbed. Rolling his eyes heavenwards, he added:

". . . made up of poor creatures who have lost their way."

"And the H is for . . .?"

"Homeless," he said.

Chapter Eleven

"I HARDLY RECOGNISED YOU WITHOUT YOUR GUN"

Jim found his cattle some distance along the track from where he had left them. He rode on to them very cautiously, then skirted round them on the uphill side. They already seemed to be camped for the night, so he lit himself a fire in front of a big hollow tree some distance back up the track, and gave Andy a nosebag of chaff and bran which he had got from Spur.

Jim sat dreaming by his fire. He knew he would have to work for wages till he had saved enough money to buy some brood mares and mate them with a good stallion. He would have to build better yards, and fence some of the limestone country. He must earn enough to make his house nicer, to make the whole place beautiful for Jessica.

Rain poured down during the night, but Jim took refuge within the hollow tree. Meanwhile, unbeknown to him, Harrison's team of searchers had found some shelter in a derelict mountain hut.

At first light Jim was on his way again, his small mob all intact. Once more the day broke fine.

He watched the cattle streaming down a steep, rocky gorge where dwarf snow gums grew, watched their horns tossing and shining in the first rays of light, their white legs trotting, trotting through the scrub. As he rode along the last high ridge before turning down towards the plains, he saw snow on the rugged skyline again—a sharp, fluted, cutting edge of snow against the sky. Jim was filled with happiness as he imagined Jessica and Spur setting out for the homestead in Spur's rattle-trap cart.

He was taking his cattle by a shortcut that he knew, so he did not meet Harrison's search party. In fact he was well below them, as were Spur and Jessica, by the time they found the note he had left for them at the fork in the track. The cattle were going quite well . . . twenty head, in good condition. Smiling to himself, Jim wondered if he had done that old rogue, Spur, out of a few feeds, and whether, as a result, there would be a lot more wallaby stew.

The cattle moved along steadily and, to a casual observer, Jim might have been asleep on his horse. The horse himself watched the beasts, and if one started to move out of the mob, Andy moved a little to one side too, just enough to give the beast a warning message and turn it back in again.

Jim was in fact wide awake. He was well aware of what Andy was doing, well aware of the value of this mountain pony which Spur had given him. He wished Jessica were sitting up there behind him now, enjoying the droving, enjoying a job well done. He thought of the warmth of her body close to his, of her face pressed into his back as they rode along, and then he wondered if any two people before had ever had such happiness as had been theirs in that circle of snow gums, below the high mountains.

The clouds were moving over the sky again, and there would be more rain. He wondered if Harrison had found his note yet. Surely Harrison would be fairer to him, from now on. He gave his cattle a quick count again—two, four, six, eight . . . yes, twenty. All present and correct. He dismounted and put on his oilskin. Another couple of hours and he should be yarding the cattle, just before dark, he reckoned. Spur should have Jessica home by then, too. The rain started to fall, softly at first, then heavily.

As it neared the homestead, Spur's spring cart slowed its hectic pace. Sheets of water lay in the paddock, reflecting the homestead lights. Then wind-driven scuds would come, distorting the bright reflections.

Jessica and Spur were huddled together under a single oilskin coat. Jessica could see the old miner looking uneasily around him, and knew he was anxious. Then all the dogs started up a wild barking, and she saw her aunt and Mrs Bailey come out on to the verandah.

As Spur pulled up his rough cart, and Jessica sprang down, they were clearly so relieved to see her that, for the moment anyway, all else was forgotten. Spur was also relieved when there was no sight or sound of Harrison, and when Rosemary told them that so far there had been no sign of the rescue party.

Rosemary insisted that Spur tie his horse up under shelter and come in for a meal, and then insisted even more firmly that Jessica should be put straight to bed. Jessica protested, afraid she might not be allowed to see Jim when he arrived.

Rosemary was adamant.

Though Spur's hut had been warm and comfortable the night before, with the sound of the wind in the trees and the rain tapping against the windows, Jessica had to admit to herself that she was tired, that she was suffering a delayed reaction to her terrifying night on the cliff. The mystery that she had yet to fathom seemed like a quicksand in a nightmare. The only certainty now was Jim, the strength of his arms and his body, his honesty.

In her bedroom, with its muslin curtains and rose-patterned carpet, Jessica was tucked into bed by her aunt. The girl demanded:

"Why haven't I ever been told about Spur?" When Rosemary made no answer, Jessica's jaw set in pure Harrison determination. She would no longer be fobbed off, she thought.

"Was my mother unfaithful?"

"Of course not," Rosemary said.

Jessica persisted.

"Was she?"

Then Rosemary simply asked:

"What did Spur tell you?"

"Nothing," Jessica answered, and she looked steadily at Rosemary. "Aunt Rosemary, please."

Rosemary looked steadily back. Then she sat on the end of the bed and took a deep breath.

"About twenty years ago," she said, "two brothers fell in love with the prettiest girl in the district. She was young, and life for Matilda was like . . . like a game." She paused for a moment. "Well, both men wanted her hand in marriage, but she couldn't choose between them. So she told them that the first one to make his fortune would be her husband. Barely serious, she sent them off like knights of old. She hadn't the faintest idea of the chain of events that she had set in motion." Rosemary paused again.

Jessica was sitting with her arms clasped around her knees, listening to her aunt as though she were a child listening to a fairy tale.

Rosemary went on:

"One of the men scraped all his savings together and gambled in one bold throw. A horse called Pardon, in the Cup. It won at fifty to one. He was suddenly a wealthy man."

"Father," murmured Jessica. "And Spur?"

"Spur," Rosemary said sadly, "went seeking gold."

In the kitchen, Spur was just finishing a chicken dinner. He felt a great satisfaction. No one would have realised that he had had an excellent meal of Harrison steak only the night before: rather he gave the impression of just having had his first good meal for months. Pushing back his plate, he got up to warm himself at the stove, and to chat to Mrs Bailey, who was busily preparing Jessica's supper tray.

Spur was clowning:

"My dear Mrs Bailey, tell me—by what magic did you transform a humble farmyard bird into such delicate ambrosia?"

Flustered, Mrs Bailey muttered:

"Oh, you do go on."

"You gave me my favourite piece, too," he said, looking wicked. "A nice plump breast."

Mrs Bailey tried to move past him, but he lunged at her, stopping her with his wooden leg. Giving him a hefty shove, Mrs Bailey set Spur firmly down on a bench in front of the fire.

"Ah, you're a cruel woman, Mrs Bailey," Spur said mournfully.

Mrs Bailey had known Spur from a long, long time ago, and she should have had an inkling of what would happen if she showed him any concern. When she asked if he were all right, Spur, who had been playing possum, made another grab for her and this time pulled her down on to his knee.

Suddenly Spur became aware that someone had come in the door and, as he looked up, he saw Jim.

"Didn't expect you yet," Spur almost growled.

Jim grinned cheerfully.

"So I see." He turned to Mrs Bailey, who, her white cap somewhat crooked, had sprung up and was attending to the tray. "How's Jessica?" he asked.

"She's fine . . . and she'd be even better if only this old galoot would let me get her supper ready."

The door from the main house opened, and Rosemary stood there, obviously startled to see Spur still in the kitchen. She did not know when to expect Harrison, but felt that, since Jessica was back, he might return at any moment.

"You'd better not be here when your brother gets back," she said to Spur.

"We're on our way," he said. "I'm too old to play the prodigal son." Bowing to Mrs Bailey, he thanked her gravely, and then turned to Jim. "Come on, Jim."

"After I've seen Jess," Jim said.

123

"I think we'd better get going." Spur deliberately emphasised each word.

Jim, after sharing those hours in the mountains with Jessica, now remembering vividly her words: "I hung on till you came", and the feel of her soft body in his arms, had acquired a new confidence. He said:

"We'll let the weather clear a bit. I want to see her."

But now, with the weather fast closing in, the search party was in fact returning up the flat towards the homestead. Too anxious to get home to care how wet they got, the stockmen cantered through the water, sending up great sprays. Harrison himself was far ahead of the others.

Jim walked along the corridor to Jessica's room, the unfamiliar feel of his boots on the carpet reminding him that this was Harrison's homestead, and that Jessica, who had only yesterday been in his arms, there below the snow-glitter on the Ramshead Range, was Harrison's daughter. He knocked gently on the door. Every nerve in his body, each throbbing pulse beat responded with thunder, as he heard her voice.

He stood shyly in the doorway. Jessica's bedroom was not an enchanted snow gum grove, with everlastings flowering in the grass. Jess was there though, sitting up in bed, her face eager, eyes dancing, and shining dark hair brushed loose all round her shoulders. She held out her hands to him.

He was just stepping forward, his eyes alight with tenderness, when there were heavy footfalls on the verandah outside, and the French windows flew open. Harrison, with water running off his oilskin, burst in.

Jim froze into stillness. He saw Harrison's austere, lined face wearing an expression which he had never imagined possible—a mixture of deep anguish and love. Then Harrison was at Jessica's bedside, throwing his arms around her:

"Forgive me," he said, in a voice that was breaking.

Jim knew that Jessica had been desperately hurt by her father, but—except for a fluttering thought when Spur said he'd look after her like his own daughter—he did not know the extent of the hurt. Now he knew how much she loved that hard, jealous man. He saw her arms tighten around his neck.

Jim heard Harrison say with a thankful sigh:

"You're back."

Jessica looked across the room to Jim, and Harrison, following her glance, saw Jim for the first time. As Harrison slowly stood up, Jim took a couple of paces into the room. The French windows were still open, and the scent of rain on the eucalypts' leaves wafted in. Jim was a born bushman and could receive a kind of benediction from that scent.

"Jim saved my life, Father," he heard Jessica saying. But he knew from the stern look quickly setting in on Harrison's face that the cattleman still saw him as a station hand, with no right to be in his daughter's bedroom—and a hated mountain man at that.

Harrison seemed to force himself to speak:

"My thanks to you for my daughter's safe return."

Jim nodded.

Then Harrison spoke in a much friendlier tone:

"Kane speaks highly of you. Says you'll make a good cattleman one day."

"I've put your twenty missing beasts in the yards," Jim said briefly.

"Maybe I could be of some help to you." To Jim's surprise, Harrison sounded really friendly now. "It's about time we had a talk."

Jim was truly amazed at this change of tone but he was willing to give this new Harrison a go. It all sounded rather hopeful.

Kissing Jessica on the brow and urging her to rest, Harrison led Jim out of her room.

Jessica leant back against the pillows. Surely her father would be decent to Jim now. He was so relieved to have her home—and she would not have been home at all if it had not been for Jim. Surely, surely, her father must accept him now.

Harrison led Jim into the sitting-room. As he turned

around to face him, Jim saw at once that Harrison was no longer looking friendly. He seemed to be thinking deeply, perhaps making up his mind about the best way to put Jim firmly in his place.

The windows were closed, and the room was stuffy. Jim felt oppressed by the chintz and velvet furnishings. He saw the piano and thought of Jessica playing it.

Then he was told curtly to sit down. This put him at another disadvantage, because Harrison then remained standing.

Suddenly Harrison's eyes snapped. He looked at Jim very hard and said:

"When did you find Jessica?"

Jim felt the antagonism, and sensed immediately the implication of the question. Jessica had been away two nights. And if he said that she had spent last night in Spur's hut, that would cause trouble too.

"Yesterday morning," he answered.

The cold voice proceeded:

"You are fond of my daughter?"

Jim felt the blood rushing to his face. All the tumbling emotions of the last few days, all the joy, choked him. At last he burst out with the words that had been running through and through his head as he drove the cattle down through the mountains:

"I love her."

Harrison spoke quietly:

"Love?" Then with a sudden vehemence, he spat out the words:

"It's a god-damned strange sort of love."

Jim stood up, unable to remain seated any longer. Harrison went on:

"Would you call it love to take a girl that has been brought up to all this," and the wave of his hand encompassed the station as well as the velvet curtains and luxurious chairs, "and put her in a bark hut?"

"We'd make do," Jim said firmly.

"You'd live on air, I suppose." Harrison's voice was

frigid, scathing. "While Jessica grew old with hard work and childbearing."

Jim found himself getting angry, but he kept his feelings well under control, all the time wondering how far Harrison would go in his taunts.

"I'd look after her. Anyway, why don't you ask her?"

Harrison's voice became even colder:

"If you'd a spark of manhood in you, you'd know that the best thing you could do would be to walk away."

"Now, just a minute, Mr Harrison!" Jim could no longer contain his anger. "You're not the only one who can make something out of life. I've got plans for my own place."

Harrison was now deliberately goading Jim, as if he wanted to see the boy lose self-control:

"Then make your plan with someone else's daughter. I didn't carve this place out of the bush to see Jessica run off with the first fortune hunter to come along."

It was too much for Jim.

"You bastard," he yelled, clenching his fists and stepping forward.

Then another voice broke in:

"Jim!" Spur spoke in a tone of command.

Jim faltered, as Harrison whirled around and stared at Spur, at first disbelieving, then furious.

Only just keeping his fury under control, Harrison shouted at Spur:

"How dare you come to this house!"

"My long lost brother." Spur's tone was mocking, and then it hardened. "I hardly recognised you without your gun."

"Get out!" Harrison roared.

Drawn by the noise of the argument, Rosemary and Jessica were standing in the doorway. Jim heard Jessica saying:

"A gun! Why a gun?"

Rosemary put her arm round her:

"Come on, Jessica. Back to bed."

"No!" Jessica almost shouted. "I'm sick of the secrets in this house. I want to *know*."

Harrison was still sternly in command.

"Jessica!" he ordered. "Get back to bed. And both of you," he said, pointing at Jim and Spur, "get off this place or I'll . . ."

Spur broke in:

"Or you'll what? Blow off the other one?" He reached down and tapped his wooden leg.

With a quick glance at Jessica, Rosemary spoke sharply to Spur:

"Spur!" she pleaded. "Please!"

Jessica was looking from her father to Spur, an expression of shock and bewilderment on her face. Jim felt stunned. Harrison had lost much of his appearance of command and looked somehow smaller.

"I only shot to warn you off," he said.

Spur laughed shortly, and rolled his eyes.

"I'd hate to be around if your intentions were serious."

Jim, feeling suffocated in the stuffy room, had an uncomfortable flash of insight into the possible repercussions of the scene between himself and Harrison, had Spur not interrupted. He saw that Jessica was almost crying, heard her urge:

"Father! Tell me what happened."

"Go to bed, Jessica!" Harrison roared.

But now Jessica got angry too, and shouted:

"No. I've a right to hear the truth."

Rosemary spoke firmly:

"Oh, for heaven's sake, Harrison, let's clear this up, once and for all." She turned to Jessica, and before Harrison could stop her, said: "Spur gave your mother a wedding present. A young colt. Old Regret's first foal. But your father couldn't stand another man giving her anything."

Harrison muttered, almost to himself:

"I wanted to shoot it, but I couldn't."

Spur said quietly:

"I'm glad to see you draw the line somewhere."

Rosemary ignored their bickering and went on:

"Your mother was afraid that something might . . . something might happen to the horse, and she turned it loose. Spur saw it running free, and came to tell her. Your father found them together. It was all quite innocent, but your father was in a rage . . . Spur was shot . . . Matilda talked of leaving your father—"

"Enough!" Harrison roared, and he strode from the room, slamming the door behind him.

"In a way she did go, of her own accord," Rosemary looked sadly at Jessica, "when you were born."

Spur had turned to Jim.

"You are entangled in this story, Jim, more than you know." He, also, was looking very sad: "Matilda's colt is now the old stallion."

Suddenly Jim pieced things together, remembering the words he had heard, perhaps when he was only a child, about the colt from Regret, and, more recently, words about the brumbies being back after years, then the brumbies coming for Bess, his father being killed . . .

"Oh," Jim said, and heard the ache in his own voice: "Of course, the leader of the brumbies." He could see that magnificent stallion rearing against the moonlight, see, in his memory, the likeness to the young colt. He could see everything now, the profound sadness of it all, yet balanced against this was the joy he had found in Jessica's love.

Spur was talking to Jessica but Jim hardly heard him:

"Who's to judge a man the rest of his life for one impetuous act?" Spur said. "It happened a long time ago. I want to forget it . . . I bear no malice." He took a step towards Jessica, who was crying softly.

"Jess, don't worry about what's past. It's the beginning, not the end." The old man prayed that he was speaking the truth.

As Jessica hugged him, as Rosemary, also with tears in her eyes, embraced him too, Spur clowned and laughed, claiming he had not had so much affection from females for many years. Then he skilfully steered Rosemary from the room and left Jim and Jessica alone together.

Jessica's face brightened, and she held out her hands to Jim.

Jim looked at her with profound longing, but made no move towards her. How could he tell her that her father had just called him a fortune hunter? How could he tell her that some of the things which Harrison had said had some bitter truth in them . . . that life in the mountains would be hard for Jessica, as it had been hard, finally, too hard for his mother . . . A bark hut instead of all this comfort . . . it was all right when a girl was young, healthy and without children, but . . . "If you'd a spark of manhood", Harrison had said . . . somehow he would have to make good. He had no words with which to explain to her.

"I'm going, too," he said, very quietly.

Jessica clung to him. She could still hear his voice ringing out, calling her father a bastard, still hear Spur saying: "Or you'll what? Blow off the other one?" The nightmare seemed to be closing in.

"Then I'm coming with you," she said.

Jim looked at her solemnly and with all his love.

"No," he said. "It couldn't work, Jess."

He kissed her—and was gone.

Jess was left alone, left without the comfort of Jim's arms, the feeling of peace and security he had given her. She was left with all the unhealed sorrows that lingered in the homestead, with all her uncertainties about her father. She went back to her room and threw herself down on her bed. From far, far away she heard the neigh of a horse. She pulled up the coverlet and wept. She wept for herself and for Jim, and for that dream-like mother who could not have known the reality of love until—married to Harrison—she had perhaps learnt that she really loved his brother.

Spur had retrieved his horse and cart from the doubtful shelter of a red gum, and was now jolting along, sitting on the damp seat, staring fixedly in front of him.

He, too, heard a horse neigh, far away. Cocking one eyebrow, he shrugged a shoulder.

Just then there was the sound of galloping hooves, and he saw a horseman riding across his path. The horseman, wheeling, forcing Spur's horse to stop, grabbed a rein near the bit.

He knew only too well that it was Harrison.

"How nice," Spur said. "You've come to open the gate for your crippled brother."

Harrison, gripping the rein, snarled:

"You've said enough for tonight . . . turning Jessica against me, just as you did Matilda, years ago."

Spur sighed, and for once let the mask of the clown that had covered so much hurt slide away.

"You misjudge the girl," he said. "Just as you did her mother."

Still holding one rein, almost pulling it from Spur's hands, Harrison rode up close beside him.

"Whose child is she?"

"Poor Mr Harrison!" Spur jested.

"You owe me the truth."

"If you had really known Matilda," Spur said, serious now, "you could never ask that. Of course Jessica's your daughter. But you don't deserve her. You'll ruin her life, just like you ruined Matilda's, just like you'll finally ruin your own." And he plucked the rein from Harrison's hand, slapped it on to the horse's rump, and trotted away.

From far away, a horse neighed again. Spur shivered, as if a ghost from the past was stalking him. He wondered if his brother had heard the sound too.

Harrison sat for a moment staring back at the lights of the homestead, and at the lights reflected in the sheets of water. Jessica was his daughter—if Spur spoke the truth. She must marry a decent man, and there must be many grandsons to carry on . . .

Chapter Twelve

"And Had Joined the Wild Bush Horses"

The fire was only just alight in the barracks, and a lantern was flickering, fading, as Jim packed his swag with all his possessions. He looked around the long, low hut, thinking of everything that had happened since his unhappy first night there, only a few weeks ago. There was the lonely sound of a cow lowing in the distance as he put another log on the fire. Then he went quietly over to Frew, who had been tossing in his sleep, and pulled a blanket over him. He walked back to pick up his swag just as the door was kicked open, and Curly and Moss staggered in, drunk and aggressive.

"Ah, Bandicoot. You movin' up to the big house, eh?" With a leer, Curly turned to Moss: "Maybe he broke in more than the colt while he was up on that muster."

Suddenly Jim's mood swung from sadness back to the fury he had felt with Harrison. Harrison and this bloody, dumb horse breaker were total bastards. He began to move forward.

Curly was too drunk to notice the clenched fists, and went on:

"Did yer have to use yer spurs, boy?"

Crash! Jim's fist connected with Curly's jaw, sending him staggering back against the chimney. He collapsed on the stone hearth, the rum bottle which he was carrying shattering. Jim stood over him.

"You've got the mind of a sewer rat, Curly," he said, just as Moss sprang at him from behind, pinioning Jim's arms to his sides, in a gorilla-like hug.

Curly was getting up, his eyes on Jim, the jagged neck of the bottle held menacingly in front of him. But the silence was suddenly broken by the sound of a bullet being pumped into the breech of a rifle. Curly stopped dead, staring into the unwavering muzzle of a lever-action Winchester. It was pointed directly at him by Frew, who was sitting straight up in his bunk.

"Throw away that bottle, Curly!" he commanded.

Curly was weighing up the chances of Frew shooting, when Frew said:

"I've done it before. So help me, I'll do it again."

With a snarl, Curly threw the broken bottle into the fire. Frew seemed to think that the odds were more or less even then, and he unloaded the rifle, but still sat up, watching with narrowed eyes. While Curly kept his eyes on Frew, Jim managed to drive an elbow into Moss's kidneys and the big bully doubled up with pain.

Jim didn't waste any time. With punch after punch, he drove Moss the length of the barracks, finally dropping him. But Curly had picked up a chair, and now he smashed it down on Jim before Moss had even hit the floor. Though the chair glanced off the upright of a bunk before it hit Jim, he got sufficient of the blow to send him reeling, and give him a return picture of a few of the stars he had seen when he came off the colt.

As Curly stumbled drunkenly towards him, Jim, still lying on the floor, kicked his legs from under him. Curly collapsed. Even then Jim waited till Curly got up and was ready. Jim knew how to fight. It took one more punch to lay Curly out.

In the now quiet room, Jim picked up his swag. He turned to Frew:

"It's a big place, the mountains. A man can be real hard to find up there," he said. "You're welcome at my fire any time, Frew."

Giving Jim a nod of thanks, Frew lay back on his bunk again, a look of pride on his face. He recognised worth, he told himself, when he met it. He had backed the boy; the boy acknowledged him as a friend.

Jim walked out into the night alone, and all his misery came sweeping back in a great tide. He went to get Andy from his stall. The horse was warm and dry, looked well fed. He nuzzled round Jim's neck and face. A sob shook Jim, and he leant his head for a moment against that good mountain pony.

But it was time to go. He saddled up and mounted. Slowly he rode out past the homestead. The only light shone from Jessica's room. Drawing rein, he sat for a second, gazing at it, then turned away and rode on.

A faint light came from the sky, where a half moon occasionally showed through scudding clouds. Jessica, coming too late to the window, could only just make out the shape of Jim and his horse. Watching until she could see him no longer, she wept, as her mother had so often wept, in those months before Jessica was born. Not once had Jim looked back.

Back in the barracks, Curly and Moss were feeling bruised and sore, albeit slightly sobered. Going outside to cool their heads in the night air, they limped towards the stables and the colt's yard. Then Curly tripped. Cursing, he bent and picked up the stone over which he had nearly fallen, and hurled it towards the colt's yard. There was a snort, and the sound of trotting hooves—and an idea began to take form in Curly's drink-sodden brain.

"That bloody horse," said Curly. "Worth a thousand pounds. Got any idea how much bloody money that is, Moss?"

"Yeah," Moss growled, his head aching from drink and from Jim's punches.

"Yeah," Curly mocked. "That's more than you'll earn in a lifetime, working for that slave-driver,

Harrison." He spat the taste of blood out of his mouth, and thought bitterly of the beating Jim had given him, of the loose tooth he now had, the eye that was already half-closed.

"I'll fix him," he mumbled. Opening the yard gate, he went inside. He could just make out the shape of the colt against the white of the rails as he ran at him, flapping his arms. The colt, terrified, rushed round the yard.

"Garn, you bastard!" Curly moved just quickly enough to turn him out the gate, and away went the colt, the thousand pound colt from old Regret, free in the dark of the night, with a hundred miles, or more, of mountains on ahead.

The beautiful thoroughbred, alone as he had never been before, nervously dropped his pace to a trot, and then to a walk. But he had heard that call of his half-brother, and he went on, seeking the horses that ran without bit or rein.

"Fixed him," Curly said triumphantly.

"Who?" Moss was bewildered.

"The Bandicoot, you idiot. They'll all think he did it."

In the morning, Kane could not believe his eyes. The colt's yard was empty, the gate wide open. The boss would have to be told at once. Kane shivered in anticipation.

Harrison was in a cold and horrible fury. He called Curly to saddle up his dappled-grey immediately, and he rode out, following the tracks as best he could. But there had been so much water, there were so many tracks. It was hopeless. He turned back, and when he reached the yards again, he ordered Kane to send messages to all the nearest stations, asking for help. Curly, Moss, and the rest of the stockmen were sent galloping off. Then Kane and Frew rode out, determined to find the colt before he got too far.

Harrison went to the house. Mrs Bailey saw his face, dark as thunder clouds, and quietly disappeared into the store room. Rosemary, looking grave and tired, met him outside Jessica's room and held up her hand in protest.

"She's cried herself to sleep," she said. "Please leave her. You've done more than enough damage already."

"Damage!" Harrison was furious. "That bloody mountain boy has left the colt's gate open."

"I'm certain he wouldn't do such a thing," Rosemary said. "But I wonder what you did to him—and to Jessica?"

Harrison strode out of the house, muttering to himself.

Kane and Frew returned late, very tired and somewhat dispirited. Harrison met them at the gate.

"It's definite," Kane said. "We found clear tracks. The colt has joined the brumby mob. They weren't far away." He paused as Harrison threw his hands up in the air. "Well, at least he's not been stolen," he added firmly.

Harrison's bitter voice cut across him:

"Somebody let him loose, and there's no prize for guessing who."

Though Kane did not agree with Harrison's inference, he did not argue. He had seen Curly and Moss that morning with black eyes, cut lips, and knuckle-marked cheekbones. He knew that Frew had seen or heard something, but the old man was not saying a word, simply growling if anyone made any suggestive innuendo about Jim. So, Kane, keeping his thoughts to himself until he felt more certain, simply said:

"Every man from every station nearby will be here by morning."

"Did you find Clancy?" Harrison asked.

Kane shook his head.

"You've got to get him," Harrison said, his voice rising. "The man's part bloodhound."

Then Harrison, his shoulders bowed, started to walk slowly away. So the last colt from old Regret had joined his half-brother's brumby herd. First Matilda's colt had gone wild, and he had lost Matilda. Sixteen years later, the brumbies had come down from the bush again—and that blasted mountain boy. And now the boy, no doubt to pay him back, had set the colt free, let the colt go to join the brumbies. Another colt from old Regret running with the wild bush horses . . .

And now he might lose Jessica's love—ruin her happiness, Spur had said. Harrison barely heard Kane calling out:

"We'll get the colt back, Boss."

It was dusk, and as Spur was returning home from the town, minus one gunny sack of gold samples, he heard the neighing of one of the brumby mob, which was making its way across a bare ridge against the sunset. They were a long way away, making upwards. Spur felt sure now, had felt pretty sure all day, that he had heard them the night before, as he left Harrison. A shudder ran through him, and he told himself firmly not to be a superstitious old fool.

Years ago, the brumbies coming on to this side of the range had seemed to be linked in everyone's minds with Matilda's death. When they had returned, sixteen years later, they had brought death to Henry Craig, and near disaster to both Jim and Jessica.

But really, when it was all boiled down, Spur reflected, the fact that old Regret's first colt was the leader of the brumby mob was Harrison's own fault. Spur sighed. He hoped that Jim, with his youth and his courage, might turn the tide of misfortune that seemed to flow in the old stallion's wake—and win out against Harrison's ruthlessness. Surely sheer courage could turn luck in one's own favour.

Still some miles from his hut, he met Jim unexpectedly, and they made themselves a campfire in the bush. Spur decided not to mention having seen the brumbies earlier that evening. He knew that Jim had misery enough without knowing that the stallion who had caused his father's death was close by. Throwing another log on the fire, he looked at Jim out of the corner of his eye. The boy was leaning back against a log, staring moodily at the dark bulk of the mountains against the evening sky.

Spur, thinking how the gold that was twenty years too late to bring happiness to Matilda might help her daughter, pulled out a flask, grabbed their two mugs and poured a good tot of rum into each one. He held a mug out to Jim.

Jim gave a start. He had been far away, thinking about his father, hearing again his voice saying: "Nought and nought still equals nought."

He shook his head.

Spur's eyebrows shot up.

"You don't drink with your partner?"

Jim looked at him suspiciously.

"Partner?" he queried.

"The gold mine." Spur waved his mug. "Your father always had a half share in it. That share's yours now."

Jim laughed. It was his first laugh since Harrison got back to the homestead, and Spur was glad to hear it.

"D' you reckon there's enough gold in it for two, Spur?"

Spur smiled.

"You'd better have a drink—it may be all you ever get out of the partnership," he said, as though the gunny sack he had left at the bank had never existed.

"In that case I will." Jim laughed again, and they raised their two mugs, laughing together.

"Here's to the gold," they said in unison. As they raised their heads to drink, they both saw a figure standing close by in the firelight.

"Clancy!" Spur gasped. "You'll give me a seizure one of these days."

Clancy stood in the firelight, grinning at them.

"You never could hear anything else while you were doing the talking, mate." His sweeping smile took in Jim. "Good evening, Jim, I thought I'd find you here, staring at the mountains."

"Yep," said Jim. He had sprung to his feet in deference to Clancy, but his voice was very quiet.

"How come you're up here?" Spur asked Clancy. "Aren't you heading the wrong way?"

Clancy shook his head.

"No. Headin' back to Harrison's."

Spur sounded mocking.

"You sure are a demon for punishment."

Clancy turned to Jim, and said:

"Somebody let Harrison's colt go."

"What!" Jim gasped, the gold mine forgotten.

"Not *the* colt—from old Regret?" Spur was shocked out of his jesting.

"Yes. The men seem sure, from the tracks, that he's joined the brumbies." Clancy looked at Jim again. "I thought you might want to be in it."

Jim sat down again, silent. His last meeting with Harrison was all too fresh in his mind.

"Well," Clancy went on, "they tell me you're good with a horse." He caught Jim's eye. "What's the first thing you do when a horse bucks you off?"

"That's easy; you don't let him beat you, you get straight back on," Jim answered automatically.

Then he stopped short, as he realised what Clancy was driving at.

"Well?" Clancy asked, and Spur echoed him: "Well?"

"No, Clancy," Jim said.

Clancy spoke quietly but very distinctly.

"Well, that's a shame . . . Harrison's blaming you for it."

Jim looked straight at Clancy, their eyes meeting and holding while the fire shadows played over their faces, and shook his head.

"Why?" Spur asked sharply.

Jim shook his head.

"It's asking too much of a man."

"Man, did you say?" Spur spoke slowly.

Jim suddenly felt as if he was being put on the defensive. It wasn't fair—they expected him to help that bastard, Harrison, who had turned him off the place . . .

"That's what my father raised me to be," he said angrily.

Clancy nodded:

"Yes, he was a good man, your father. Maybe it's just as well. Harrison probably wouldn't let you ride with us anyway."

Jim sat frowning into the fire.

The fences of Harrison's yards showed faintly in the dawn light. There was movement at the station . . . Horses, like dark shadows, were tethered to rails, to hitching posts, were standing in yards, all moving restlessly. There were horses being shod: there were horses snuffling and stamping in the cold. Men moved purposefully, saddling up, buckling breastplates and cruppers, strapping on oilskins in front of their saddles, filling nosebags, buckling up saddle pouches and quart pots . . . all the cracks had gathered to the fray . . .

As the light strengthened, breath of both men and horses hung in white clouds. Men and horses were everywhere. A treecreeper's pipe heralded the dawn, and then a magpie carolled. One kookaburra laughed, another joined in, till the dawn chorus rang around the homestead, drowning the sounds of neighing and snorting, the creak of leather.

As voices became more cheerful with the first rays of the sun, the horses' coats took on their different colours—chestnut, grey, bay, black, roan, liver chestnut. Men began to discuss their horses, and examined with interest ones which they had not seen before. The cracks now formed themselves into groups, joining up naturally with old friends whom they knew well. Even some of the mountain men who had been at Henry Craig's funeral were there, the men who had been determined that Jim should earn the right to be a mountain man.

There were young men on thoroughbreds, dressed in narrow-legged, white moleskins, and there were even men from further away, who ran their cattle and sheep on the sunlit plains. Some men wore rough leather leggings, some wore sheepskin coats. Paterson, having got word about the colt, had managed to arrive in time.

Eyes kept looking towards the mountain. Through all the movement there was a rising beat of excitement.

Harrison jumped agilely up on to a wagon, and addressed the waiting crack riders. In contrast to the vivid excitement in all their faces, his face was strained and drawn.

"Gentlemen," he boomed. "I appreciate the speed with which you've responded to my call. My colt, the colt from old Regret, is running with the most cunning mob of brumbies that ever crossed the ranges. I've positioned scouts to send up smokes as soon as the brumby mob is sighted . . ." He broke off as heads began to turn, and exclamations began to break out in the crowd.

Clancy was riding down the track towards them. Harrison waited, his face expressing something like relief.

"Thank you for coming, Clancy," he said, even before they got close enough to shake hands. "I need your help."

"I'm ready," Clancy said quietly. But he seemed to be waiting for something.

There was another horse approaching at the canter, and Harrison recognised both Jim and his horse.

"Look at him," he said with black fury. "Come to survey his handiwork, I suppose. Kane, get that boy off my property at once."

Clancy spoke firmly:

"If he'd done it, he wouldn't be here."

"Do you really believe that?" Harrison's voice was full of scorn, and he looked at Jim, who had pulled up a little distance away and now sat perfectly still and straight on his horse. Both he and Andy were dirty and tired-looking, for they had travelled far in the last few days, but, travel-weary as they were, Jim still had an air of dignity and pride, as did his little horse.

The crowd of riders had gathered a little closer, every ear straining, as Harrison again ordered Kane to get Jim off the property.

Then Clancy raised his voice and spoke sternly, clearly.

"Just hold it a moment!" he said. "Both he and his horse are mountain bred. I think he should come along." He stared Harrison straight in the eye. Here was Harrison, the boss, and Clancy, the great rider, the tracker, the legend, and neither of them were going to give way.

"We don't need *him*!" Harrison's voice was cold and cutting.

"I asked him," Clancy stated.

"You did what?" Harrison's tone was of disbelief.

Clear and strong, Clancy's voice rang out.

"I want him along."

Harrison wanted his colt, and he needed Clancy.

"As you wish," he said finally. "He'll dig his own grave."

Clancy rode up to Jim.

"You'll ride with me," he said, loud as a whipcrack, for all to hear.

"Yes sir," said Jim, gathering up his reins. A small smile passed over Clancy's face.

Men were swinging into their saddles, all around the yard. Harrison spoke again, from his horse now, standing in his stirrups:

"Gentlemen." He paused to get their attention. "There will be a reward, to be divided among you as you like, when the colt is recovered—one hundred pounds."

There was a cheer and all the riders pushed forward to the gate—thirty horsemen thrusting to get through—eager, bumping, jostling. Men were laughing, calling out to each other, urging their horses, knees and shins squeezed between saddle flaps and the next horse's shoulder or flank. All around was a seething, tossing wave of horses' heads and manes—grey manes, black manes, chestnut, red, silver—the horses toey with excitement, bits jingling, stirrup irons clashing.

In the dust and the clamour, Jim was seemingly unaware of the three women standing on the verandah—yet his every nerve ending registered the fact that Jessica was standing there. Now the gateway was clear, and he shot forward at the gallop, towards those sharp and rugged mountains, leaving behind the slab and shingle house, the brilliant creepers on the verandah posts, the smoke from the chimneys . . . and the girl.

Voices rang out ahead of him, men laughing, men chiacking each other about their prized mounts, the cracks already becoming one body of men, with a thrilling current flowing between them—each one of them seeking the colt who had joined the wild bush horses that ran unbridled and carried no weight.

These men were seeking one thoroughbred colt in all that tangle of bush, amongst all those precipitous gorges, cliffs where early snow lay in the sheltered crevices, and amongst the maze of ridges leading to the white-crowned peaks. Some were riding for the fun of it—for the wild excitement, both for the rider and his horse, of rounding up brumbies, chasing the swiftest quarry a horse can chase. Some were determined to retrieve an immensely valuable colt; some wanted to be known as the best and boldest riders, and to show off as well the excellence of their horses.

There was one who was out to be the hero, to take home the reward, so that no one would ever suspect that he had been the culprit.

And there was one who burned with love of the mountains, and with the memory of the girl he had held in his arms below those snow-capped peaks, who had to prove himself worthy of that girl, who burned too with the memory of his father's death, which he now had a chance to avenge.

At last he could earn the right to be a mountain man—a strong, enduring mountain man.

This rider was young enough not to count the risk, and to thrill to every thundering, flying, pounding moment of the gallop.

Chapter Thirteen

"Clancy Rode to Wheel Them"

Whisper of wind in the black sallee trees, rattle of a pebble falling from the rock outcrop high above — the black stallion's ears flickered as he grazed on the snowgrass. He raised his head, ears pricked forward, listening, waiting, listening. A nervous ripple ran along his hide. There was something...? The bush was too quiet. He looked up at the rocky outcrop, but saw only the rock itself jutting out prominently, the blue sky, the outline of treetops.

Then, bursting from the trees beside the rock, came a flight of black cockatoos — huge birds with eerie, wild, echoing screams, flying with their characteristic sling-winged action over the herd. This time their blizzard cry must surely be a warning of something different.

Two men, hidden by small snow gums, were on the rock, scanning the bush, watching, waiting, listening. One had knocked that pebble down; otherwise they were silent. But the black cockatoos had seen them.

The brumby stallion stood there while his herd, only momentarily disturbed by the birds, grazed around him in the glade. He stood quite still, even though he could feel the skin down his back tighten at the scream of the black cockatoos, and he waited.

A little further back, small spirals of smoke rose from the fires at which the crack riders had been boiling their quarts and eating some lunch, all the time waiting, watching, waiting.

Jim had tethered Andy a small distance away and was standing with him, alone. With his quart pot buckled back on to the saddle, Andy's girth tightened again, the reins now hung loosely over Jim's arm. Clancy rode up to him, his eye all the time cocked for a signal, and asked how Andy was going, after the long distances they had travelled.

"He's raring to go," Jim answered, patting the intelligent dun head with the dark ears beside his shoulder.

Clancy began to move on.

"Thanks for your help," Jim said, looking up at him with gratitude.

Clancy had a half grin on his face as he cast his eye across the horizon again.

"Now!" Clancy suddenly shouted in excitement. Then, spurring his horse into action, he took off, vanishing like a genie into the bush, with a scurry and clatter of hooves, and a kick up of dust and pebbles.

Jim swung into the saddle and followed him, as a shout went up from the group of men around the fire, and they rushed for their horses.

"It's on, boy," Jim whispered as he leant along Andy's neck. He felt the elation surge, beating with every pulse beat, in time to the horse's cantering hooves, and to the hoof beats of those who were catching him up, passing him, or well behind. His senses were now absolutely keen: he was sharply aware of his hands gentle on the reins, of his thighs and knees strongly against the saddle, of his intimate contact with the horse beneath the saddle, of the calves of his legs against the horse, and his feet firm in the stirrups. He felt such fine communication between himself and the horse that he knew almost instinctively at any moment exactly what Andy was thinking, feeling.

The thoroughbred stallion, watching and waiting in the black sallee clearing, heard a sound afar off. He stood, head flung up to the wind, his ears alert, every long, soft hair transmitting its message. Then, trotting around his grazing herd, he moved them towards a gap in the dense trees. He looked up once towards the mountain skyline, through that gap, then back to a treeless place on the ridge behind him.

The sound that he had heard was clear and close now, a thundering drum beat — the sound of galloping horses. Was it another mob of brumbies? With another, younger stallion? Then the horses and their riders topped the ridge.

The black stallion swung round with a snort and drove his mob, full gallop, out through the gap in the trees.

A shout went up from the riders. Clancy had seen the colt among the mob; Jim had seen him too, and he had seen Bess, still with the headstall of her bridle around her neck.

Away went the brumbies, with thirty horsemen after them. Harrison gave a yell to those behind, urging them on.

The riders split into two groups, aiming to encircle the herd. Clancy led off on the northern wing, that side of the ridge where the undergrowth might be a little thinner, Harrison following him, also Jim, and Curly, and one of the mountain men. Harrison's face was set in lines of grim determination. *This* colt must not escape. Leaning right over his grey's neck, Harrison was galloping through the trees as though to beat his great destroying demon — the flaw in his successful life that had renewed its force with the return from the mountains of that black thoroughbred brumby stallion.

Jim was taking his horse carefully, trying not to tire him early in the chase. He leant forward, keeping his weight off Andy's quarters, saving him, feeling every movement of that little dun as part of himself. He was looking far ahead all the time, always picking the best line to take.

Clancy, the leader, though much more used to riding the plains, knew well how to gallop through the bush, and he was looking ahead too, so as to avoid getting "yarded" by an impossibly high log, or encountering thickets of saplings or wattles that would slow them up.

Horses' hooves pounded on the damp ground and rang on the stones. Occasionally the hooves thudded on timber, as a horse did not rise quite high enough over a fallen log.

They were gaining on the brumby mob. Jim could see it up ahead, its racing, flickering shadows through the tall straight trees, and the black stallion there, behind the herd, forcing on the pace, heading for the mountains that he loved.

Clancy's big brown was faster than all the other horses, even Harrison's dappled-grey, and he soon outpaced them, gaining, gaining on the thundering herd. The pitch of excitement seemed electric through the forest. The drumming beat of the hooves throbbed through every horse and rider — throbbed through the brumbies too, so that they went faster and faster.

Andy never faltered, never put a foot down on a loose stone, or knocked a tree trunk when they jumped. His dark legs moved with perfect timing, lengthening a stride where a longer stride was needed, leaping logs without effort, absorbing every change in the terrain into his own rhythm. Jim leant forward, thighs firm against the saddle, talking to him as they flew through the flickering trees, never waivering his attention from the rough ground ahead.

On, on, they all galloped, leaves whipping hands, legs, faces, the strong hop scrub sometimes wrenching a rider's foot from a stirrup iron.

Clancy's brown was drawing well ahead, and Jim could see him galloping alongside the mob. The black stallion was leading the brumbies now, and the young colt, his half-brother, was not far behind.

"Head them! Swing them, Clancy!" Harrison called, as he urged his grey to go even faster, but Clancy could not have heard any voice above the thunder of that herd, and Clancy, the legend, knew what he was doing.

They were neck and neck, Clancy's brown and the grand old stallion. Jim, still nursing Andy along, was not far behind. Harrison's dappled-grey was streaking forward, the frenzied excitement of the chase having seized him almost as furiously as it had his rider.

Then Clancy was passing the black stallion, riding him off, heading him, and at that moment Clancy started cracking his whip. Halting the herd, swinging his great spirited horse in front of the swirling mass of brumbies, Clancy cracked and cracked his whip, and the echoes sounded—a hundred or a thousand echoes—off the mountains all around.

Clancy held them. Poised there, on his brown horse, smiling, Clancy held the mob. Then there appeared the great black stallion in front of Clancy—that stallion so enormous, so overpowering, out of the deepest dreams of all mankind, stood rearing there, confronting the audacious, skilful man who dared to try to hold him, the horse raised to his fullest height between his herd and the legendary rider on his magnificent horse.

Then the stallion dropped back on to his four feet and, responding to his bold act of defiance, the brumbies were surging towards Clancy, who momentarily lost the upper hand. And when that black stallion, looking towards the mountains he knew so well, threw up his head and trumpeted a wild neigh, he led the mob, full gallop at Clancy, and they were able to swing under his whip, and take off with renewed speed—stallion, colts, mares, foals, fillies.

Harrison on his grey sprang in to protect Clancy from being swept underneath the stampeding mob, and to try to head them off, but the brumbies were pushing Clancy aside, their bodies, black, chestnut and bay, pressing against his legs, buffeting his horse, paying no heed to his whip, racing away, heading for the mountains—and taking Harrison's prize young horse, the colt from old Regret, with them.

Jim sped after them, keeping a little to one side, knowing every ridge and gully, trying to imagine himself as that brumby stallion, determined to escape, and trying to anticipate that horse's every movement.

They came to some open country, and the brumbies were racing over springy tussocks of snowgrass, the horsemen close behind. They entered a stand of straight-trunked trees, and those wild horses became for a time like spirits, like dancing shadows, except for the pounding sound, and there, among those trees, they gained a little more on the horsemen.

One rider, over-keen, went on one side of a tree and his horse went on the other; another fell off as his horse stumbled on landing after jumping a log, and was dragged by his foot caught in the stirrup until his boot twisted free.

What a wild steeplechase was this, with the only steeples the tall, tall trees, and the prize a colt worth a thousand pounds!

Curly was riding near Jim, and Jim could tell that the larrikin intended to be the hero of the day, if he possibly could.

More open country lay ahead. Clancy was still in the lead of the crack riders. Jim looked back once, as he left the trees behind him, and saw Barty Paterson jumping a big log in perfect steeplechasing style. Close beside him, Curly was spurring on his horse, and yelling. Jim had no intention of pushing his horse yet. Far worse country was still to come—thick timber, rivers, gorges, and cliffs. Curly could ride to win, at the start of the day, if he wanted to.

They came to a strip of country which had been badly scarred by a very hot bush fire that had killed trees, felled others, and burnt right into the roots and the earth, making the ground rotten. Grey logs lay at all angles, sometimes with stiff grey branches sticking up, and the earth was uncertain for take off, uncertain for landing. The brumbies, without the impediment of riders on their backs, gained ground here, as riders fell amongst the red soil and the charcoal and the bleached grey logs.

Jim, without forcing Andy, was getting closer to the lead. A few strides on loose earth, then over a silver log: a lengthening stride, a perfect landing beyond a hole: another log, and another jump: another landing.

Wattle scrub had sprung up along the edge of where the fire had burnt. Curly's mate, Moss, coming up towards the front of the chase, ducked under one fairly solid branch, only to be hit across the face by another and to be pushed backwards off his horse.

Jim drew rein for a quick assessment of the country and of the brumby stallion's likely next move. He turned his horse in a full circle once, taking in both pursuers and pursued, and then struck off in a different direction, seeing a shortcut he guessed might be useful. Curly followed him, still whipping his horse on with the handle of his stockwhip.

Jim now saw that he had guessed right, for the brumby mob appeared suddenly in front of him and wheeled to cross a wide, rocky stream. The horses were almost hidden by the great spouts of water which splashed up as they plunged through the river, as they leapt over boulders and crashed off bars of rock.

As Jim and Curly raced to follow the herd through, alongside each other, the water glittered, and the spray bit into their bare flesh like ice. When they scrambled up on to dry land, Curly spurred his horse past Andy and, leaning over, grabbed the headstall of his bridle and wrenched it over the horse's ears.

Jim, completely taken by surprise, raised his hands a little to keep the bit in Andy's mouth and raced on, still keeping well up with the brumbies. With Curly riding fairly close, Jim now realised that he had more to deal with than simply the chase.

The brumbies cut across a point where the tea-tree grew thickly, its paper bark hanging, creamy white, and headed to cross the stream once more. When, at the water's edge, Curly came right up beside Jim again and made a swift lunge, aiming to knock him out of the saddle, or remove his bridle completely Jim knew for sure that Curly meant to put him out of the chase for the colt. Jim also knew that river, had seen the deep hole upstream from the shallow bar of rocks across which they rode; he now realised that there was only room for one of them on the rest of that journey and that he must ride Curly off as though he were a bullock breaking from a mob. With grim determination, he manoeuvred Andy's shoulder up against the other horse's shoulder, his own leg crushing against Curly's, the horses flank to flank. They rode like this, almost locked together, halfway across the wide stream. Curly sensed the danger but in a flash his horse had stepped sideways before he could do anything to prevent it. Suddenly the larrikin and his horse had rolled into a deep river hole.

The water was foaming around boulders which in the coming frosty days would be encased in ice. Jim splashed and bounded his way through them, barely pausing, only looking back for long enough to see that Curly was not drowning. The furiously gesticulating larrikin bobbed up, leapt to his feet, slipped and went under again; meanwhile his horse had already scrambled up the bank and galloped away, its reins trailing and broken.

By no chance could Curly recapture Harrison's colt and be the hero of the day, but Jim was still only holding the bit in Andy's mouth by the reins. It was necessary for him to pull up, dismount and put the bridle back on. As Jim struggled with the buckle of Andy's chin strap, all the crack riders still left in the chase went thundering past. Jim could not conceal his agitation, because suddenly he wanted—wanted desperately—to catch that brumby stallion, that bearer of grief. And now all the others had raced past him.

Quickly, the bridle was on again and Jim had swung into the saddle and was away, galloping up long grass glades and down into ferny gullies, along ridges where the tall trees grew. The cracks were now thundering close behind the galloping brumbies but Jim, still quite a long way back, was gaining on them as he felt the breath being almost pounded out of him by Andy's pounding strides. His stomach muscles were taut, his thigh muscles gripped tightly, his whole body felt strong, and his surging blood beat time to the quickening pace.

All the riders were strung out now, galloping across

the gently tilting plateau. Jim had been in that part of the mountains before and he knew what lay beyond the highest point. He realised that here was the mob's last chance of shaking off their pursuers because that plateau's edge dropped away as though broken off, and below was an unbelievably steep and rocky slope. Sure-footed brumbies could make their way down that slope but riders would only dare attempt it at risk of their lives.

Realising that the moment of truth was to come, the cracks spurred on their horses. With Clancy still in the lead, they galloped right to the verge and saw the brumbies vanish before their eyes, leaping over the plateau's sharp edge. And there, at the very edge, they pulled their horses up short, on their haunches—a row of horsemen gazing aghast at what lay below.

Chapter Fourteen

"THE MAN FROM SNOWY RIVER"

Jim, eighteen years old, his father dead, his home somehow no longer his, his job lost, his girl denied him — yet with his own horse and those intangible gifts with which his parents had endowed him — galloped up towards the line of crack riders.

Jim knew that precipitous mountainside down which they were looking; he saw the fallen timber, the myriad wombat holes, the scrub, the saplings; and he realised all the dangers they presented. But as he saw all the cracks halted there, gazing helplessly at the brumby mob galloping down that steep face, a fire of excitement exploded within him.

Suddenly Jim galloped straight through the watchers without a thought. His horse shouldered Harrison out of the way as the words "bloody bastard" formed in his mind, jumbled and faded.

Then he swung his stockwhip in a mighty arc and gave a triumphant yell, and Andy, his great-hearted dun, leapt over the plateau's edge. Horse and man were airborne . . . treetops coming towards them . . . scrub, rocks.

Jim felt Andy land without faltering, just sliding a

little on the steep earth, and then they were galloping down a slope like a wall. Some big trees stood upright, straight and tall, but mainly that incredible mountainside was covered with scrub. Wombat holes riddled it, fallen logs lay criss-crossing it. There were rocks that moved beneath hooves, and there was loose earth. Jim leant back, taking his weight off Andy's shoulders, and had only enough hold on the horse's mouth to help him, should he stumble. In both man and horse there was one driving force — to catch that herd of horses that were galloping, sliding, stumbling, swerving on ahead.

A bleached, grey tree trunk lay right across their path. Jim collected his horse, pressed him on to the bit, and somehow, even on that steep slope, Andy gathered his legs under his body and leapt.

Jim eased his weight more forward for the jump, felt as if he, too, were lifting the horse. He had to guess the degree of slope on which they would be landing, and lean back... and they were away again... that unimaginable gallop... the strong movement of his horse beneath him... the air rushing past and the trees flying by... scrub grabbing at his legs, whipping his hands, forcing itself between his knees and the saddle. The earth was sliding and crumbling under his horse's hooves, and the angle was unrelentingly steep.

The group above watched in amazement.

Harrison sat with his hands tensely gripping the reins, his eyes never leaving the galloping dun below, the lines on his face carved even more deeply than usual. He knew that the boy rode with death.

Clancy, sitting on his horse beside Jake, the leader of the mountain men, was watching keenly, and there was a look of pride on his face. Jake's lips were pursed, and a faint whistle escaped him.

Paterson, the dreamer of dreams, the myth-maker, the composer of bush ballads, watched and saw all from that brink. He saw the mountainside, dropping straight below their horses' hooves. He saw the brumbies galloping, unfettered, through thick scrub, saw rocks rolling under their hooves, saw them swerving to miss saplings, leaping logs, jumping down small rock faces, half-falling into wombat holes: and he saw Andy, the dun horse, small and wiry, flying that mountainside behind them. He saw Jim, the mountain boy, riding the dun, completely attuned to his every movement — to the little horse's rhythm — riding him so that his own body's weight would never throw him off balance.

Ahead of Jim, the herd of brumbies reached the bottom of that terrible descent and vanished into thick scrub, among tree ferns, bracken and blanketwoods. Through the wall of scrub they crashed, and then they were gone, and the scrub closed behind them.

Jim reached that rough valley floor himself, with no time to marvel that he and Andy were still alive... The brumbies... the brumbies? He could hear them ahead. Fern fronds whipped him, whipped Andy across the face. They burst through the blanketwoods, beyond which were thick-growing young mountain ash, almost too thick to penetrate. Just keep with Andy... almost lie along his neck... don't be knocked off by a tree... turn toes right in... press your legs into him...

The smell of the horse rose around Jim and he could feel Andy's sweat soaking his moleskins as he urged him on and upwards, and they sped through those thick trees. He could see Andy's muscles straining beneath the dun hide, but was too excited to feel his own stomach and thigh muscles aching.

Trees flashed by... such a gleaming white trunk... bark streamers hit his shoulders... see the lowries diving through the branches... trees... trees...

Suddenly the mountain ash opened on to a clear, flat knoll. There was no sign of the brumbies. Jim pulled up and cast around for tracks, finding some, and then he heard the brumbies, and saw three or four between the trunks. They were heading down into a valley.

Through the trees, as he pounded down towards them, Jim saw the glitter and gleam of water, foaming down around rocks. There was a short, steep cliff, a slide into that water. Those riderless brumbies slid down it and into the stream. Jim could see them bounding, splashing, and half-falling as they crossed the water. By then he had reached that red clay slide.

Without hesitation, Jim put Andy at this slope, leaning right back as he slid down on his haunches, front legs extended, front legs meeting the water first, meeting rock. And then they were leaping, plunging, splashing, and leaping again, till they were across the ice-cold river.

On the other side, Jim lost the tracks, and there was no sound of brumbies. He saw two narrow, grassy gullies that twisted and turned through a forest of mountain ash and turned Andy up the left hand side. They had only gone a few yards when the brumby stallion burst round a corner, straight for them. For a moment, it seemed as if the huge stallion would gallop over them, then it swung away, upwards, the herd following, and Jim — pushing Andy now — was after them as hard as he could go.

Presently the woollybutts thinned out and then there was a bare hillside ahead. It was there, on that bare hillside, that Paterson saw them, still galloping upwards towards the shining snow. Paterson watched, amazed.

"He's with them still," he whispered, under his breath, and the other cracks sat their horses in silence, watching the distant herd, the small and distant horseman, all fade from sight.

Jim and his horse went on and on, down into tangled, matted gullies, up on to ridges, on into the snow gums. They were approaching a place where he knew there was always a great drift of wind-dropped snow. The pace had become slower, and he was gaining on the brumbies. He could hear Andy blowing; he was gasping for breath himself, and sweat was running down his face and back. Andy had almost turned black, he was so soaked with sweat.

There at last was the huge snowdrift, and there was the great stallion bounding, and plunging, surging his way across it, white snow flying around the black horse, the whole herd following, each horse surrounded by its own cloud of spray.

Jim, as he galloped towards the drift, was watching the stallion, and the horse's magnificent beauty struck him afresh. The thought went through his head, pounding in time to the pounding hooves: "Matilda's colt: he's really Jessica's now . . . but he owns himself . . . the wind and the mountains own him, too . . ." The picture of the unbridled, unweighted stallion plunging through the snow was vivid in Jim's mind's eye, as he and Andy began leaping and ploughing through the deep, soft snow behind the kicked-up snow of the brumby mob.

In that deep snow, Andy faltered, he half-plunged head-first, he half-fell. Jim saw the cold and smothering snow: he saw the blue lights in it and the golden glittering reflections, but he held the horse's head up firmly, seemed almost to pull Andy up on to his feet. And away they went again, plunging and ploughing through the snow.

The brumbies, without the weight of riders, had gained on Jim and the dun. They burst out of the snow, spray flying from their coats, from their manes, from their tails, and were galloping on snowgrass and through the wind-twisted trees well ahead, but Jim, with his own breath rasping in his throat, his face and hands tingling, stinging from the snow, knew that they were tiring. He knew that here, on the snowgrass ridge, he must turn them, wheel them, head them, and hold them.

So Jim urged Andy on, till he was passing the mares, the foals, the fillies, the colts, passing Bess, passing the young colt from old Regret, and then neck and neck with the great black stallion. Jim could hear the stallion's sobbing breath, see the whites of his eyes . . . beautiful horse, surely not the bearer of grief . . . That dream . . . the horse both good and evil, night and day, love and hate . . . the blizzard wind, and the falling snow . . . Jim was ahead, swinging round him, and he and the stallion stood squarely facing each other — proudly facing each other.

Presently, and without taking his gaze from the stallion's eyes, Jim rubbed Andy's withers, whispering:

"Well done, well done."

Then it was time to raise his whip with a commanding crack, and to turn the exhausted herd back — in the direction of Harrison's homestead.

Jim knew the job still had to be completed, and he must not let the brumbies get their second wind, must keep driving them, keep them tired — which meant that both he and Andy would be even more tired than they were. So back and forth, he rode behind them, and on each wing, cracking his whip, keeping them under control, simply keeping them going in the way he wanted them to go.

Pictures still kept floating into his head, disconnected pictures such as he had seen during the wild action, and he saw that great, black stallion, in his memory and his mind, standing in front of him — that stallion who had been partly to blame for his father's death, but with whom he shared the blame, the stallion whose trumpeting call in the night had foretold disaster, yet whose noble body was at one with the mountain blizzard, the seed in the wind.

Slowly Jim's mind began to think more clearly. He was very tired, but still there was a job to finish, the herd to control, Bess to give back to Spur, the colt to return to Harrison. He summoned up all his reserves of determination and so on they went towards the homestead.

Pools of sweat had formed beneath the bellies of each of the crack riders' horses as they had stood in line watching at the edge of that drop. But in time the sweat had begun to dry, so that there were just long, dark streaks down shoulders, rumps, and hocks — and furrows of sweat and dirt on the men's faces. At last, well after they last caught sight of Jim still following the brumbies, they began to turn for home.

Jake's face was set, and no one could tell exactly what he was thinking:

"If he doesn't kill himself, he'll be lost for days," he growled.

Paterson cast a last look over that unbelievable drop below them, down which that boy and his game mountain pony had galloped, and he looked far beyond, into the distance, with that vision which garners all — the giant trees, the snow-etched range, the vanished horseman and the wild horses... the courage... the untamed Snowy Mountains.

Harrison was the last to leave.

"Hot-headed young fool," he said, but there was a tinge of admiration, almost envy, almost sadness in his voice, and in the last look that he cast backwards.

The cracks rode very slowly back through the quiet bush, rather quietly and thoughtfully, for how could a boy succeed where all of them — grown and experienced men — had failed? The riders who had fallen, or dropped out for one reason or another, were found along the way, including Curly who had managed to find and catch his horse; they were a bruised and chastened lot, wet, but mainly unhurt, with a horse or so that had cast a shoe or was going short. And somewhere, way out in the mountains behind them, a courageous mountain boy was still running a mob of brumbies on his own.

Spur had driven to the homestead soon after the musterers had left to run the brumbies. He had arrived with a bottle of champagne, one of his purchases in the town, and had stayed on, stating that the women needed a man to look after them.

When the dogs started to bark, it was Jessica who first ran outside on to the verandah, but Spur was close behind, with Rosemary and Mrs Bailey. Then they saw the distant group of riders and no mob of brumbies in front of them. Spur suspected that it was time for him to go, or at least to be ready to leave; but this still unfolding drama partly concerned Spur and he, too, had played a part in its creation.

Jessica did not even notice that he had stumped off to the stables; he was out of sight as he harnessed his horse into his cart. But as he drove round to the front of the homestead and saw the expression of mixed fear, anxiety and misery on the girl's face, he simply pulled his cart up to a halt nearby, and waited, and wondered. Where was Jim? Where was that dun horse which *he* had given him?

Jessica was outside the garden gate. Her eyes had searched among those riders for Jim, for Andy — neither was there. As the riders drew closer, she called out to her father:

"Where's Jim?"

Harrison just shook his head, not even looking angry at her question.

Spur saw Jessica's hands tighten on the fence, sensed her fear, and felt a strong urge to put his arm round her — for Matilda's sake as much as for her own.

The riders, quiet and obviously tired, were almost at the yard gates when a faint whipcrack in the distance made old Frew look back:

"Glory be!" he shouted. "Will you look at that!"

Every head turned. Jessica stood on tiptoe, staring along the track. Just coming through the stand of red gums, and framed by a blue and rugged peak, a mob of horses could be seen — jaded horses, barely making a trot. Soon it was quite clear that it was the brumby herd, and that Jim and his little horse were bringing them along.

Jessica gave a shout, but then she and everyone else became silent, because they could see that the brumbies were beginning to get nervous, and feared that any noise might frighten the horses into attempting to gallop off. One or two of the men looked as if they wanted to help, but Clancy sat like a statue, a look of immense pride on his face. Jim must savour his full triumph. He must bring them right to the homestead and yard them on his own.

Spur, risking his brother's fury, sat there in his ramshackle cart, grinning broadly, watching every move. He looked like a man who had backed a winner — in fact he knew he had. He was also deeply conscious of the fact that Jim's courage and his understanding of the stallion, and of the mountains to which they both belonged, had swung the luck from evil to good.

Jim was still having to work hard to hold his mob together, riding to and fro behind and on each wing, cracking his whip, making sure that he and his weary, sweat-stained horse were always in the right place to hold the mob and keep it going.

"We've just got to get them this last half mile," he murmured to Andy, "and then yard them. We've got to do it... We'll have earned the right to go home to the mountains then... Make the house better, for Jess... build yards and paddocks for brood mares and foals... have to break in the young ones of this mob..." He looked ahead, assessing the likely difficulties of driving a mob of wild horses through the gateway to the main yard. "Try to get Bess in the lead," he thought. "Or perhaps, better still, the colt. He knows the place well, but either would lead the mob."

His whip arm was aching, his legs and knees aching, Andy felt tired beneath him; but they drew closer and closer to the yards, closer and closer to that well-built homestead which was Jessica's home, but was also the house where Harrison had called him a fortune hunter. He could see the brilliant chrysanthemums in the garden, but even as he took in the pink and golden flowers, he kept his attention fully on his mob.

They were nearly there. He could see all the cracks sitting, tensely waiting. A few more yards... The colt and Bess were going up nearer the lead and Jim flicked them both neatly on the rump with the lash of his whip, just enough to make them leap forward, ahead of the big stallion. Then Jim and Andy closed in, whip cracking, driving the mob hard. At the gate, Kane grabbed the colt from old Regret by the headstall, and Bess led all the others into the yard.

Harrison was standing in his stirrups, keenly watching the performance. Paterson, eyes bright with excitement, sat on his horse, absorbed in the whole scene, and absorbing all. Clancy's smile was broad and contented.

Jim ran the mob through the gate into the yard and followed them in. He closed the gate; then he patted Andy, leant forward and whispered in his ear:

"Well done, boy. We've done it."

There was a rising murmur of voices which Jim hardly heard. He perceived the brumby mob in the yard, but in his mind was a vision of his home below the snow-etched peaks. He rode quietly through the swirling mob to catch Bess and, for one proud moment, caught the gaze of the black stallion and triumphantly returned it; then he took Bess by the bridle.

Kane held the gate so that Jim could lead Bess out from among the agitated brumbies, and take her across to Spur.

Kane was dodging heels and hooves, trying to hold the colt steady so he could inspect him. The foreman wanted to check for any damage to those fine legs, which had not really been bred for country as rugged as that through which the colt had just galloped, but the young horse was wild with nervous excitement. Jim, with no change in his serious expression, rode back to them and spoke quietly to the colt he had broken in, quietening him for Kane and Harrison to examine, then handing the leading rein to Kane, and moving away.

Harrison walked towards him. It took a moment for the cattleman to speak.

"Craig," he said at last, "I promised a hundred pounds. It's yours." He held the notes out in his hand.

Jim, standing very stiff and straight, shook his head.

"That's not why I rode," he said.

The cracks sat on their horses in complete silence. Somewhere down by the creek a plover called, his cry plaintively suggesting reasons that Harrison would never know — Jim's father's death, his longing to live on his own mountain property, to prove himself a mountain man. But there were reasons, too, which Harrison knew full well.

"There are a dozen good brood mares in that mob," Jim spoke again. "I'll be back for them." He looked beyond Harrison straight into Jessica's dancing, happy eyes. "And for whatever else is mine."

Harrison turned to look where Jim's gaze had gone, and saw Jessica.

"I don't like to repeat myself," he said. "She's not for you."

"Jessica can make up her own mind about that," Jim replied firmly.

Even Harrison could not be furious. He had seen courage and skill, and determination, and he knew it, and he recognised a quality in Jim which he had never had himself — a gentle quality, the ability to give happiness and create trust.

"You've got a long way to go yet, lad," he said, but his voice had more than a touch of respect. Jessica had moved a little away from her father's side.

Old Spur spoke up from his cart:

"He's not a lad, brother. He's a man."

Then Clancy, the legend, sitting on his horse, debonair as ever, touched his hat in salute, and said:

"The man from Snowy River."

As Jim raised his hand in a silent greeting to Jessica, Barty Paterson, who would one day be Australia's favourite balladist of the bush and its people, whispered to himself:

"The Man from Snowy River."